No man is an island
by Brian Staff

A collection of short stories on three dimensions of life

No man is an island by Brian Staff

A WordisWorth book
First published in print in 2008
Printed by CreateSpace

No man is an island is also available as an ebook

Library of Congress Control Number: 2008920583
ISBN 978-0-9802474-0-4

Editor and designer:
Alison J. Macmillan

A note from Brian

Have you ever found yourself thinking the whole human race is a bunch of idiots? Do you ever reckon it would be infinitely better if everyone thought and behaved just like you?

Well I've got some news that you might not appreciate: most people are just like you; they're merely coming at the situations that aggravate you from a different angle, their angle, which on a different day could be your angle.

If you're trying to make your journey through life a little easier, it's best to start at home, looking at yourself. Next, introduce others into the mix and look at the interactions, not just from your side, but from theirs. Then, stand back and look at the whole mess we call life, look at it objectively, and you'll realize that some things can't be fixed, they just have to be dealt with.

This collection of short stories looks at life from these three angles – the person and their personality, how it can shift and change; the social animal that has to deal with family, friends, co-workers, strangers; and the odd situations that just come out of nowhere and leave us scratching our heads in bewilderment. You might guffaw, groan or cringe as each story brings the joys, conflicts, challenges, nonsense and meaninglessness of life alive, and provides a surprise ending. I aim to give you a witty and entertaining look at contemporary life and experiences - here are some highlights:

In *Turning 50*, a wanton drunk turns the tables on a dour comedian whose life and jokes are sometimes indistinguishable. *Heart and Sole* was described by *Writers' Forum* as "hilarious" and "a clever insight into the rules of conduct when shopping with your other half" when they awarded it first prize in a short story competition.

In *Liar*, we are invited into a hot and heavy relationship with Sally, a mistress of tale telling, who points out the holes in any criticism of her by showing that lying is just part of everyday life. *The smell in the bathroom* reminds students, groups and professionals alike of the rough and smooth of sharing living space with others - an individual proclivity can test the tact of the best, and turn a run-of-the-mill existence into an exercise in diplomacy.

This collection provides insight into the human condition and is for people who want to enjoy a good read and take time to laugh, rather than engage with a self-help manual to get through life's dysfunctions.

Each story has a moral, and it's up to you to decide what it is. Take a couple of minutes at the end of a story to think about its message, and, if it's useful, how you can learn from it, because learning about yourself, others, and how to cope with the unexpected, might make this "vale of tears" just a little more bearable, and maybe even fun.

The fact you are reading this is down to my wife, Alison, who has pulled her finetooth comb through all of the stories to knock out errors, fix things that didn't make sense and improve readability. She did all the illustrations, provided the extra quotes, phrases and snippets, and formatted it for publishing.

It's lucky for me that she loves to laugh - even at herself. If it weren't for Alison, I would not have had the necessary life experiences to write some of the stories! Thank you, Alison: soul mate, best friend, and life partner.

Brian

Fathering sin, and The art of meditation

Brian has completed two further novels, which will be published in 2008. We can let you know when they are available. Just send an email to: alison@WordisWorth.com.

Fathering sin:

Have you killed anyone lately? Are you sure?

Fathering Sin concerns a boringly normal man, Phillip, a computer geek, more functional with logic than with people and their illogical problems. When a sequence of murders takes place he feels linked to them. Unsettling visions possess him, hurling him into a mental breakdown, his decline encouraged by his son, a frightening and menacing presence, lurking at the margins of Phillip's life.

Simultaneously, the crime detective, the careworn Spencer, yields to a bizarre relationship with his superior officer. Her attitude towards both the case and Spencer verges on the merciless and feeds off the gruesome crimes they are trying to solve.

Fathering Sin turns the usual ideas of life and death on their head.

The art of meditation:

Peter is a political cartoonist and a dyed-in-the-wool cynic (an invaluable characteristic for one in his profession). When he finds himself at a meditation center in the depths of rural Wales, he struggles to take it seriously, and spends most of his time meditating on (and drooling over) a young woman he meets there. But the bizarre deaths of two of his fellow retreatants cause him to see the place in a different, ominous light and he gets drawn into a confrontation that quickly moves from the philosophical to the physical, causing him to focus more on saving his skin than his soul.

No man is an island
The collection

Part 1 - Your life

A wanton drunk turns the tables on a dour comedian, whose life and jokes are sometimes indistinguishable. Contains never-before-heard comic monologues.

Part 2 - Life with others

Trials and tribulations of sharing a space. After reading this, you will never again complain when your housepartners forget to take out the trash.

Coupledom is great, but one size may not fit all.

Is it ever alright to lie? Sally thinks it's a part of life, but her partner no longer knows what to think.

As your relationship progresses you learn more about your partner, but you may try to hide a few facets of your personality. Sometimes, though, things are better out than in.

Household chores as "relationship counselling"? If sparks fly when you and your partner embark on a joint project, read this and learn how to calm the waters.

Part 3 - Just Life

Describing someone without being offensive is simply expected etiquette. But the good old government of the US of A may need a visit from Miss Manners.

How many words do you know? How many do you need to know? Are the words you know the same as the ones I know?

However we justify it, the act of killing an animal may live with us until the end of our days. D. H. Lawrence said it all.

Have you ever seen a fitness fanatic with a smug smile? Come with me on the journey from hobby to obsession and back again.

Sickness is as much in the mind as in the body, and your idea of my sickness may not agree with mine.

Do you throw a fit when your computer freezes on you, but just shrug your shoulders when a relationship breaks down? Get some perspective!

Part 1 - Your life

Turning 50

My fiftieth birthday. Time to take stock.

The table in front of me is littered with a half-empty bottle of wine, a half-full pack of cigarettes, and a half-finished Chinese meal.

The wine will get finished, and almost certainly a new bottle will be started, and maybe finished. Likewise the cigarettes. The Chinese meal? I won't eat any more of that. I'll crush the two forlorn-looking fortune cookies in my hands before I have a chance to read their messages. "Your life will be full of peace and joy." "You will meet the love of your life." Fuck that.

Fifty years. A failed marriage and countless failed relationships. Well, I guess they must be failed, otherwise I would still be in them, wouldn't I? I still can't work out why my ex-wife hates me so much. Our time together went from liking to loving to despising in the course of a year. Maybe I should enter us for the Guinness Book of Records in the *speed to hate your husband* section.

The wine bottle is empty. How did that happen? The next one is open, and no sooner is the synthetic cork out of the bottle than I'm fiddling with the cellophane on the next pack of cigarettes. Fingers that fumble over the most rudimentary of tasks seem to find no problem with extracting corks or unwrapping cigarettes. I'm even having trouble writing these days, particularly signing my signature. The *S* for Steve is okay, well, it would have to be, after all what is an *S* but a squiggle? I get the *Pet* part of my surname done, but then my hand seems to freeze in a state of rigor mortis. My brain tries to help out and urges my numb hand to get on with the *erson*, but when brains start messing with things that we've programmed ourselves to do naturally, it just doesn't work out, makes matters worse in fact, and I end up just slurring the final characters onto the paper in an illegible mess. My signature ends up looking like how I'll pronounce my name when I've had my first stroke, which can't be that far off now. Perhaps my signature is trying to tell me that; give me a warning that if I don't lay off the bad habits and develop some good ones I'll soon be saying my name in the sad blurry form that I currently write it.

Fifty years old, and what the heck have I got to show for it? Less hair, more fat, fewer brain cells, more deficiencies and deformities, less fun. Even an evening like I'm having tonight might have been fun 30 years ago, on the assumption that by the time I was 50 things would have gotten themselves into shape. But no. Things, like my body, are as out of shape as ever. Worse than ever. Ever worse.

I make coffee, not because I want it, but just because I can, or at least I think I can. I hope I still can. It tastes like vomit. Sour and unnecessary, but I drink it anyway, like a man in a desert drinking his own piss, because it's there and because it's wet.

The room is getting thick with smoke. It's cold out and I have no intention of opening a window, and anyhow, I live in San Francisco, so if I open the window it will set up a competition between the pollution without and the pollution within, carcinogen fighting carcinogen for supremacy, for the right to get into my lungs. If I smoke enough maybe the contents of the room will disappear from view and won't be able to accuse me any more. Everything is accusing me. The wine and the cigarettes for obvious reasons. The coffee because it tastes so goddam awful. The food because I haven't eaten it, and if I packaged the remains up and sent them to Africa they would probably save someone's life.

I don't really feel as if I'm the worst person in the world. Actually, I have a sneaking suspicion that I'm the best person in the world, and it's the fact that nobody realizes it, least of all me, that is making me so screwed up. For example, I'm sure that if my wife had thought I was the best person in the world our marriage would have gone on a lot longer, maybe as much as six months longer, or as long as it took her to find out that living with the best person in the world is just as hard, if not harder, than living with one of the dregs of humanity.

I look at my hand and see a fresh cigarette in it. By stubbing out cigarettes very carefully it's possible to make 30 butts fit into the space that would normally be occupied by 10 or so, thus making my consumption appear to be far less than it actually is. I've also mastered the art of diluting the amount of wine I drink. I don't mean actually diluting it by adding water. I mean diluting it by reducing the number of units I consider to be contained in a bottle of wine from six to four. I've done this in two steps over time. I cut it down from six to five when I first heard that the Europeans had medical evidence that drinking wine can be good for you. I couldn't let that news go by unnoticed, could I? Then when I heard that the Americans were endorsing this finding, I immediately dropped it from five to four. After all, the Americans hardly ever believe anything anyone else says (they didn't believe Hitler was a bad guy until he'd toasted a millions Jews), so for them to agree, with the French of all people, was a significant breakthrough for the world, for the wine industry, and for me in particular.

Thus do I delude myself. I know it's a fix, but I can actually believe my own delusion. Isn't that incredible? No, actually it's not that incredible. In fact, it's thoroughly credible. If we all believed that the things that could happen to us were going to happen to us, the authorities would have to be pumping the water supplies full of drugs just to allay mass suicides. If we all confronted reality there would be so many bodies lying in the streets that it would be a major health hazard; people wouldn't have a clean place to commit their own suicide because of all the selfish corpses that had beaten them to it. No, reality is not for public consumption, it's just too ... well, real.

What do I do for a living? Come on, guess. I'll bet you this last glass of wine, and believe me, I'm pretty keen on drinking this last glass myself, so the stakes are high, on my part at least. But it's a safe bet for me you won't get it.

I'm a comedian, a stand-up comic. You'd never think it, nobody ever does. When I turn up for gigs, sight unseen, people don't believe I'm who I say I am. They expect jokes to pour out of me right from the greeting handshake, or at least they expect to see someone who looks as if they might be just the tiniest bit humorous, but I don't. I look like an undertaker on a bad day, my countenance is beyond funereal.

I'm not one of those comics who puts on a glum demeanor as part of the act. I really have a glum demeanor. Jokes are just my way of avoiding reality, that's why I began telling them to myself when I was a kid, just to get by. I started by telling myself jokes I'd heard, then I went on to embellish them, and I thought the embellishments were okay, so I went on to make up my own jokes, bad ones at first, but better ones later. Then I started telling the jokes to other people, the ones I'd heard to begin with, then gradually mixing in one of two of my own, then only telling my own. The day when a stranger told me a joke that I'd invented (and it was such a bizarre joke I don't think it could been invented coincidentally by anyone else), was the day I started to believe I could call myself a comedian and make a living out of it.

I was wrong.

Anyone can call themselves a comedian, but making a living out of it is a completely different kettle of fish. I'm well enough known on the comedy club circuit and I keep reasonably busy, but at my highest level of earnings I only manage to eke out a living, and for the most part I'm scraping along, storing up debt so that when a better spell comes along and my bank balance creeps stealthily into the black, most of it is sucked into repayments before I even get sight of it. I think I'm stuck in what is called the vicious circle of poverty. Any meat that I can put on my financial bones during good periods is gnawed off voraciously by the people with whom I've incurred debt during the bad ones. The only reason I'm not starving is that I have no dependents to drag me underwater for good and all.

I'm also stuck in a vicious circle of relationships. I'm attracted to women who are attracted to the funny me, because they're probably sharp and fun-loving. But when they see the other me, the majority me, they lose interest. Women who are attracted to the real me, the sad pauper, are either desperate or charitable or perverted, and none of those characteristics exist in the sort of woman that I like.

I stub out the last cigarette. I know it's going to be the last cigarette because it is, quite simply, the last cigarette that I have, and at 2 a.m. I'm damned if I'm going to take my life in my hands and visit the convenience store on the corner. Most convenience store operators live in fear of thieves, of the spaced out junkie with the Uzi who shows up in the middle of the night to take all he can get, and is so wired that he's more likely to fire off his gun than not. In the store nearest me, however, the one store that I can rely on being open 24x365, it's the store owner who does the intimidating. He's just about the meanest looking s.o.b. in the city; a white, craggy-featured hulk of a man with dirty grey hair and shaggy eyebrows that hang half way over his eye sockets, which makes you feel as if he's looking at you through parted curtains; mean, dirty curtains that shade a mean and dirty interior. He makes little secret of the shotgun that he keeps under the counter or the 9mm automatic that is sometimes rammed in the waistband of his pants. It's not only smoking that's shortening my life, it's visiting the shop where I buy cigarettes that's more of a threat to my continued existence.

I take my last swig of wine. There's more booze in the house, but it's hard stuff, and if I get started on that we're into a whole new party, and I'm just not up to it tonight. I take a last glug of coffee, but I end up spitting it out in the sink. While I'm there I decide to swill some water round my mouth, but the swill soon takes on the taste of tobacco, wine, monosodium glutamate and coffee, so I spit that out too. Standing at the sink I can see my reflection in the window. I look gaunt, disheveled, hollow-eyed, old, which altogether is about as good as I get.

●●●

Comedy is about taking life to ludicrous extremes, I tell the audience, that's why I'm a comic, because I am a ludicrous extreme.

My love life, for example, has always been full of outrageous frustrations. When I was an adolescent I took premature ejaculation to new heights. I only had to see an attractive girl to ejaculate. Then there was no point dating her because I'd already had the orgasm that all my relationships were focused on, and I could save myself the money I'd be spending on her by spending it on me. And what did I buy with the liberated cash? I bought beer and pornography of course, which made me even hornier and, therefore, even more prone to the lightning ejaculation syndrome. Girl to eyeball to optic nerve to brain to testes to prick in milliseconds. I squirted away like a water pistol with a hair trigger in the hands of a nervous tot. I was a completely self-sustaining sexual ecosystem. All I needed was visual input and my depraved imagination did the rest. In fact, I got to the point where I don't think my imagination had much to do with it any more. The warm splat in my shorts took place on sight of a well-shaped babe as automatically as a learned reaction, programmed behavior. The psychologists call it "Pavlov's Dick", I tell the audience. The smart ones laugh. The less smart ones laugh louder to show they get a joke that they don't get.

I play a club in the Castro district pretty regularly. It's a gay district and the audience is predominantly queer, but I don't change my act. I have a few homo jokes, but I don't tell any more in this place than I do anywhere else. I think we've got to the stage where gays don't like to be constantly reminded that they're gay any more. They're gay, okay, that's it, now let's talk about interesting things like do we need an oil change (that's oil in the car, not *Oil of Olay*). Even the President must like to forget he's President now and again. Well, maybe not. Not this President. He seems to be the kind of guy who really likes to be reminded that he's President, and that if he stops being reminded he'll actually forget he's President, and somebody else might say he's the President, and then the President and this new guy will have to have a televised debate where one says "I'm the President", and the other one says "No, I'm the President, dickhead!" and then the crowd squeals and points at the second guy and shouts "Loser! Loser! You called him "dickhead" so he must be the President!" I tell the audience.

Anyway, I like gay audiences. They seem warmer, somehow, and they don't interrupt. Interruptions drive me crazy. Some comics like them, thrive on them. Not me. I panic. My insecurity causes me to believe all the insults that the interrupter hurls at me. He tells me I'm crap, so I'm crap. He tells me to get off the stage, so I get off the stage. That's what I do. You yell at me, insult me. I quit. I'm known for it. People hiring me know this. It just takes one whacko in the audience and the act is over. Maybe that's why I don't get good rates. There's a 50:50 chance that 50% of the act will not happen, so I get paid 25% less than if I was reliable and they knew I was going to fill 100% of the slot, guaranteed. I don't do guarantees. I'm as-is. *Caveat emptor*.

I'm increasingly being asked to play places with older audiences. Needless to say, this is scaring the crap out of me, literally - there's no need for MetaMusil in my overflowing medicine chest. My fear partly arises because older folks are a tougher crowd. The audiences seem to be composed of middle-aged cynics whose favorite all-time movie is *Dirty Harry*, people who sit back and say to themselves "Okay, punk, make me laugh!" But my fear is mainly due to the fact that I'm mortally terrified of being labeled an "Old Folks Comic", which is about as back-handed a compliment as you can get, a bit like getting the prize on the hospital ward for being "the patient who needs least pain medication each day." I'm the best palliative on the market.

I guess the cloud has a silver lining though. As I get to play to really old folks I'll be able to recycle my material more because they'll all forget the jokes between visits. In the end I'll be playing to a bunch of geezers who are so forgetful that I'll be able to use the same jokes multiple times in a single set and they'll find it equally funny, or unfunny, each time. But by that time I'll probably be so forgetful myself that I won't be able to remember any jokes. Well, I guess if I can remember just one joke and leave a minute or two between repetitions (I'll fill the interval by playing tasteful pieces on the ukelele), I'll be able to continue to be a comic until the end of my geriatric life. Which is all a roundabout way of saying that no matter how bad it can be at times, I have no plans to be anything other than a comedian for as long I walk the surface of this generally humorless earth.

I stumbled upon this career-confirming realization that I would eternally be a comic and nothing else about five years ago. One evening, after a ton of booze and about a cubic kilometer of cigarette smoke, I had an epiphany. It was revealed to me, as if in a religious experience of the highest order, that I was doing the only thing that

I wanted to do or could do, and despite my love/hate relationship with my trade, it was my true vocation. I still think back to that crystalline moment with warmth and a wave of joy, which in my case is manifested by an almost imperceptible curling of the corners of my mouth into an orientation that is marginally above the horizontal.

It's also made my life easier. When friends used to advise me to quit my life as a starving comedian it always resulted in an anguished debate and painful soul-searching on my part. Now I just tell them to mind their own fucking business. Being a comic, they think I'm joking when I'm rude to them. That's one of the perks of my trade. You can insult people and they don't know if it's a joke or not. Needless to say, most of my relationships end when the person being insulted realizes that the jokes aren't jokes and the insults are intended, and, in some cases (my ex-wife, for example) the situation is exacerbated and the breakdown of the relationship accelerated when the person chooses to interpret even jokes as insults.

● ● ●

I met my wife sitting on a bench in Golden Gate Park, I tell the audience. It was a coincidence. I had actually gone there to hook up with a 17-year-old virgin from Palo Alto whom I'd met in an Internet chat room. I was hoping she wouldn't be too disappointed in the mismatch between the 18-year-old boy with a passion for dancing and weightlifting she was expecting to meet and the fat, balding 37-year-old with a passion for beer and East European gymnasts that she would be confronted with. If she couldn't handle the switch-aroo, I'd brought a bottle of her favorite drink with me, Starbuck's Frappuccino, laced with a product I'd bought in a shop in the Tenderloin district that euphemistically called itself a "Love Potion", but was really a sedative powerful enough to knock out a herd of frisky bull steers – she would get the Potion and I'd get the Love. Unfortunately, the 17-year-old, female virgin turned out to be a 60-year-old male pervert from Cupertino who had a passion for fresh-faced young weightlifters. After exchanging a few heated words we calmed down and actually got to be on quite friendly terms, and started discussing the sort of things that people like us discuss, such as the decline of ethical standards in the S&M industry.

But after 20 minutes or so my new friend admitted that he'd arranged a backup meeting, or "assignation" as he quaintly termed it, with a 16-year-old boy from San Jose who was big into stamp collecting and reptiles, and whom he had arranged to meet at the next bench along. We were on such good terms by then that I actually gave him my bottle of the Starbuck's laced with the Love Potion, wished him *bonne chance* and hoped that his date was coffee lover enough to swig back the Frappuccino. We laughed in a comradely way, I tell the audience, imitating the laugh. But the 16-year-old boy turned out to be a 35-year-old woman who was expecting to meet the same 17-year-old virgin that I had been expecting to meet but was actually confronted with my decrepit 60-year-old buddy. The woman was mad, but my buddy was madder and actually smashed the bottle of Frappuccino over her head and stormed off, hobbling (I don't think I told you that he walked with a cane). I sat on my bench for a while ruminating on the duplicity of humankind.

I don't know why people are so worried about Internet chat rooms. I reckon that most people in teenage chat groups are hoary old perverts pretending to be something else. The mean age of the "teenage" participants is probably around 50, with a variation of plus or minus five years, a variation that is referred to mathematically as the "standard deviation". Not many people get the standard deviation gag, because this whole spiel is delivered rapidly to get maximum effect from the juxtapositioning of the various sexes and ages of the characters, real and pretend, but the ones who do get it laugh loud to show how clever they are, making the rest feel dumb, so they laugh too and in the end it gets far more laughs than it deserves; that's the wonder of peer pressure.

Anyway, the woman on the next bench was sobbing gently as she picked shards of Frappuccino-soaked glass out of her hair, and being the warm-hearted individual that I am I went over to comfort her. We got chatting as I helped her mop Love Potion from her clothes, and we realized we had a lot in common, which was not surprising given that we'd both come to the park with the same objective. But I think the Love Potion started to work on us via inhalation (it had the unsubtle smell and volatility of gasoline), because before long we were both woozily lounging on the bench, with glazed eyes, talking as if our mouths were full of cotton wool and planning the rest of our lives together. Kismet, I tell the audience. Or do I mean Karma?

This skit, which I refer to as "Perverts in the Park" on my gag list is, I admit, near the mark for some tastes, bordering none too subtly on the verges of criminality, child endangerment, sex abuse, pedophilia, date rape, grievous bodily harm, ageism, and probably a bunch more punishable crimes. When I do it I can sometimes sense a tension in the audience, a tension that says "Should I be finding this funny? Is this guy some kind of dangerous nut? Should I storm out, lock up my kids and call the cops? But wait a minute, people are laughing. I'm laughing! Is there something wrong with me that I need to know about?" Well, I don't know for sure that this is what they're thinking, but I reckon I'm close, because it's pretty much what I'm thinking.

I don't use this piece on young audiences, who just don't get it or find it creepy. Nor do I use it on old audiences, who simply can't believe that the world has declined this much – comedy that strays too far from a person's view of reality moves into the realm of the absurd, and that's a whole new ballpark of entertainment and really not for me. It goes down best with intellectuals, liberals, yuppies, people who think they're a bit avant-garde, think they've got everything figured out so that they can walk the line between white and black, between good and evil, and always make sure they return to the right side, avoiding the dark side. If I'm feeling a bit mischievous and the audience strikes me as a little too smart, I lower the ages of all the protagonists by three years, or even five years if I'm really motoring. The more you push the envelope the bigger the laughs, until a certain point where you've gone too far, then the laughing stops and the shouting starts. Then you're in dangerous territory. Hard to get back from there. Actually, hard to escape with your body intact in some cases.

Of course, this skit also goes down pretty well with sexual deviants, and one could argue that they may interpret it as encouragement to continue or even expand their perverted ways. But if I took into account the sensitivities and predilections of every member of the audience, my gag list would reduce to one – probably something about a road and a chicken.

Let me return to the thing about the comedian picking up what the audience is thinking. Well, "Yeah, so what?" you're probably saying. "If they laugh they like it, and if they don't they don't. Easy." Well, it's more complex than that. I can tell if the audience is quiet but really enjoying it, and I can tell if they're laughing but really not enjoying it that much. Don't ask me how, but I can, and most comics who've been around a while will tell you the same. I could do my shtick with earmuffs and a blindfold and still be able to tell you how it went down. I guess it could be telepathy or something, but I think it's really more mundane than that. My material is okay. I know it is. I'm my biggest critic, and if I think my stuff is alright it's probably a damn sight more than alright. If I'm delivering it well, and I know when I am, when it's flowing smoothly and sweetly with all the emphases and intonations and cadences in the right places, then the audience picks up on that and it all works. And vice versa. I have some gags that are marginal, and if I'm in top form they work like a charm, but if I'm bad they bomb, bomb, bomb. It's just science, psychology. Comedy is as predictable as venereal disease.

• • •

I get to bed around 3.30. No matter how drunk I am I go through all the rituals. Washing my hands and face, flossing, brushing the chaotic lineup of tombstones that I call teeth for the regulation two minutes, which the electric toothbrush measures out for me. I comb what I've got left of my hair (fuck knows why I do this at bedtime, but I do). There's so little order in my life that the few things that I stick to are like havens of sanity, and I sometimes think of some gags while I'm waiting for the toothbrush to finish its tedious task.

My lifestyle is crappy. Booze, cigarettes, junk food, no exercise (the "stand up" part of my stand up comic denomination is the closest I get to a workout). But I accept that the disgusting mélange that is my life is what contributes to my ability to think up jokes. If I was a tea-drinking, non-smoking, health-food-eating churchgoer, I can't imagine that I could come up with anything even remotely funny. Of course, I'd probably be so smug about being me that I wouldn't have to retreat into self-ridicule, but frankly, given the two options, or any in between, I'm happy to be in the position at the end of the debauchery scale that I occupy.

Unless I feel as if I'm going to pass out as soon as my head hits the pillow, I know I'm going to have big trouble falling asleep, and really big trouble staying asleep. So, I swallow sleeping pills like a kid devours popcorn, mindlessly, more interested in watching the movie of my life than in caring about how much damage I'm doing to the leading actor. God bless the capitalist society in which we live, and the rapacious pharmaceutical industry that it has spawned. The fat-cat pharma folks are so keen to keep piling up the profits that they're inventing new drugs all the time, which means that people like me, who overuse one type of sleeping pill and are soon having to take half a bottle to get the same result as half a pill once provoked, can just transfer to the next drug on the production line.

• • •

Ever wonder, I ask the audience, where these exotic new diseases keep coming from? Ebola virus, AIDS, Green Monkey fever, Asian bird flu, West Nile virus, flesh-eating bacteria? When I was young we had to make do with smallpox, polio, whooping cough, tuberculosis. Really boring stuff. Kids today have so much more to choose from. This is a good thing. Right? I mean we all have retirement plans, don't we? And those retirement plans usually contain a good chunk of investment in manufacturing companies, and some of those companies are bound to be pharmaceutical companies because they make such a boatload of cash. Right? So, if those companies couldn't be sure of new diseases turning up that they can make medications for and profit from, we'd all be poorer, wouldn't we? You gotta love the good old capitalist ecosystem. We can even transform misery into money. Well, someone else gets the misery and we get the money, but there's no such thing as a free lunch, right?

I'm overweight, I tell the audience, stating the obvious. Half of you are overweight. I can't see you clearly, I tell them, shading my eyes against the stage lighting and scanning the room, but I know half of you are overweight because that's what we are in this country. There are three things that are certain in our American life: death, taxes and flab. And all three of those things are patriotic gestures. We have to die to get out of the way so that the next generation can come and get their turn of suffering. We have to pay taxes so that we can continue to terrorize the rest of the world. And we have to get fat so that we can spend a lot on food and spend even more on the drugs that we need to cure the illnesses that the food induces. Being fat is a patriotic act. Eat up, my fellow Americans! Your country needs you, and the more of you there is the better. Your flab is fuelling the wheels of countless industries.

The F.D.A. is rightly named, isn't it? I ask the audience. The Food and Drug Administration. They administer food and drugs to the population. Feeding us up like craving junkies so that our frantic consumption can lead to someone making fantastic profits. One man's diabetes is another man's Porsche.

They should make being overweight part of the qualification for getting a visa to work here. To get a green card you should need to be clinically obese, and to become a citizen you should be a waddling, slobbering, staggering blob of food and drug consuming lard! What use are those fucking skinny vegetarians that you see waving flags at the naturalization events they show on the local news channels? Are they going to help the beef industry boost consumption? Are they going to need a load of healthcare? My sister's a nurse, I tell the audience (I don't have sister). She's going to get put out of work if these healthy anarchists start taking over. She's got three overweight kids to feed and a husband who passes out if he's not chewing something that's at least 50% pure fat. We need sick people. What use are a bunch of immigrants who spend their money on lettuce and running shoes? I bet the bastards even get more than ten miles a gallon out of their fucking un-American Japanese cars! Just think of the long-term effects that's going to have on the oil companies, and I bet half you people in this audience have got investments in oil companies, and not necessarily the fat half! Come on, we built this country on conspicuous over-consumption, so over consume, conspicuously!

I don't do a lot of political stuff. In the end it's not that funny. It's tragic. Shakespeare might have done some good routines in the tragi-comedy area, but he didn't play to some of the audiences on my circuit.

• • •

Does anyone enjoy getting up in the morning? How is it possible? I've enjoyed it just a handful of times in my entire 50 years plus one day, and every time it has been a Christmas day, up until those Christmases when my stocking started holding, not toys, but things like socks and alarm clocks. Just about the worst thing relating to getting up in the morning is that first look in the mirror. I don't know how nature manages it, but somehow it contrives to make me look progressively worse every single day. When I first noticed this trend, which would have been at some time in my early 20s, I assumed that I would be looking like Quasimodo or an unmasked Phantom of the Opera by the time I was 30. But nature has been slightly kinder than that, although only slightly, and I'm sure that the inexorable progression will lead me to the height of ugliness in due course.

That first glance in the mirror reminds me that I have a big nose. Not incredibly big, not in the Cyrano de Bergerac league, but big nonetheless. Worse, I have no excuse. I have no racial pedigree that enables me to take pride from my preponderance of proboscis.

I'm not a Jew. I assume that Jewish mothers would be lining up
to marry me to their smolderingly beautiful, black-eyed, sexually
repressed daughters if I could claim that my nasal legacy was tes-
timony to the suffering of Abraham's people. But I'm pure WASP:
Whitish (I tan easily), Anglo Saxon (four generations removed),
Protestant (non-practicing), so I have no excuse. I'm just ugly.

Did I become a comic because I look odd, funny? Did the length
and breadth of my schnozzle form my career? I guess that's the
popular theory. Can you think of any good-looking comedians?
Probably not. But the comic as misfit story is old, older than me, so
it's really old.

• • •

Freaks. I say to the audience, and I pause. There will be a giggle,
maybe a guffaw. If they're really with me there may be an honest
laugh or two. Freaks. I say again and get more of the same reaction.
Our society loves freaks - pause - but only some of them. Take the
freak who takes a big stick, runs at a bar and, using the stick, pro-
pels his or herself over the bar. What a fucking useless thing to be
able to do. But the best freak wins gold medals at the Olympics in
an arcane sport known as the pole-vault, and he or she never has
to do anything else in his or her life. They can spend their entire
existence using their high-tech big stick to jump over ever higher
bars and make a handsome living out of it. Not just a living, not
just a good living, but a great living. Scientists spend time that
could be spent doing better things designing better sticks for these
freaks, time that they could have spent designing stronger armor
for troops who are out there putting their lives at risk subduing
people who aren't like us and don't like us. And when the freaks
can't use their sticks to jump over the highest bars any more, they
start lecturing half-stoned business people on how the lessons they

applied in using long sticks to jump over bars can be used to run businesses better. The transition from big stick bar jumper to motivational speaker is seamless and incurs no financial hiatus for the freak. Hasn't anybody ever told these people that if they lashed a few poles together and propped them against a bar, they could shimmy up them to clear unheard of heights, and they would only have to spend a few hours learning to tie knots, not lifetimes in learning how to pole-vault?

And there are many such instances of freaks making out. The hammer, for example. Big man with big weight on big chain throws big distance. Wow! Discus? Likewise. Shot-put? Replace the heavy iron ball with a suicide bomber and I can see the use of it. Javelin? Replace the grass where the thing lands with another suicide bomber and I can see the use of it. The triple-jump? What an extremely valuable attribute that is, to be able to hop, step and jump further than anyone else. When did you last see someone hopping, stepping and jumping as they hustled to catch a bus, or as they rushed to save a child from drowning? "Stop hopping, stepping and jumping you fucking pansy," I shout at the audience, "and get that kid out of the water before it turns blue!" And then there's the whole realm of freaks with freakishly sharp hand-eye coordination. We award the ability to hit, catch or throw a round object (aka "ball") with riches beyond belief. The average professional baseball, football, basketball, golf-ball, tennis-ball, soccer-ball player earns more in a year than ten thousand nurses in Africa earn in 68 lifetimes, more or less.

Like I said. We love our freaks.

But why is it only the faster, longer, bigger freaks that we laud? Why doesn't the guy with the below average hand-eye coordination deserve our admiration? The kid in school who walks like a gorilla, who could no sooner catch a ball than fly, who takes a couple of days to respond to a bang on the head. Isn't he or she special too? We treasure the slow love maker, why not the slow reactor, the slow learner, the slow thinker?

They have all sorts of whacky sports in the Olympics these days, like ballroom dancing. Is that a sport? I always thought ballroom dancing was a way to demonstrate how fundamentally unfair the world is, or how perverse a sense of humor God has (the two are completely interchangeable, as I've discovered many times throughout my time as a bit-part actor in this absurdist play we call life). Girls love the boys who are the best dancers and the best dancers always turn out to be gay. The girls get frustrated, the swivel-hipped boys get frustrated, and the clomping, uncoordinated heterosexuals get really frustrated, wondering why girls don't get turned on by useful and attainable things like beer drinking capacity. I'm waiting for the day when they have a gold medal for the most normal person in the world. I'd sure like to meet him, or her, or it.

• • •

It's 1 p.m. by the time I start thinking about breakfast, which is somewhat typical for me. I could eat in or I could eat out. Eating in would mean getting the low calorie version on account of the fact that I don't have any food in the house. Eating out would mean getting the high calorie version because I simply find it impossible to go to a restaurant and not order the unhealthiest things on the menu. I decide to eat out. I go to a diner a couple of blocks away where they do all-day breakfasts. No matter what time I get up, I always want to eat something like breakfast as my first meal, even if I get up at 6 p.m., and I get up at 6 p.m. more times than I would like to admit.

When I first started working full-time as a comic straight after college (straight after I flunked out of college, that is, not straight after a successful, star-adorned graduation), I found the wacky hours exciting. After six weeks or so of excitement I found the hours troubling, as if I existed in some remote hinterland that didn't relate to what the rest of the world did. My social life outside of work was falling apart because I was in bed when my friends weren't and vice versa, and given that I didn't have much of a social life in the first place, the falling apart soon degenerated into complete collapse. But I soon got over it, and ever since I've considered myself to be nothing more than a shift worker operating on the margins of a society that I could never be a part of even if I tried.

I'm in the manufacturing industry. I manufacture phrases and stories that other people hear, causing their bodies to manufacture hormones that trigger their organs to manufacture laughs. And we like to laugh. It may even be good for us, although the idea of my jokes having any wholesome purpose actually makes me feel uneasy. I certainly don't intend them to be wholesome. I guess I intend them to be vaguely troubling, challenging maybe. My favorite comics – Fields, Allen, Bruce, Carlin, Hope – all had a dark side to a lesser (Hope) or greater (Fields) degree. Not just a dark side to their personalities necessarily, but a dark side to their humor, as if every now and again they'd lob out a gag that in a slightly different setting could be quintessentially serious. "Life's a bitch, and then you die." Funny, or not.

The diner is half-full. It's always half-full, never full, never empty. I must come in here about three times a week. It's a 24x7 place and I've probably been in here during every hour and day on that 24x7 clock and it's always half-full. Sure, the customers change radically over the course of the day. If the prim women who sit drinking coffee at 11 a.m. could see the scumbags who had been sitting on the same seats at 3 a.m. they would jump ten feet in the air, and when they realized they might even have a cup or a plate or a spoon in common, they would run out of the place screaming and spitting, never to return. That's the great thing about cities. They keep you grounded, if you let them (you can delude yourself anywhere if you try hard enough). The foul and the refined are only a hair's breadth apart.

I order eggs & bacon, toast, coffee and orange juice. I order other stuff as well, but those five things are the staple ingredients that any breakfast must have. I read while I eat, which means that I eat slowly. It takes me an hour to finish eating, and by that time what's left of the eggs has congealed, and the bacon fat has come out of the hiding place it goes to when hot, and is now clearly, greasily on show. I love it. I believe food increases in taste as it ages, right up to the point where it develops mold, and in some cases beyond, as with cheese, for which the mold stage is the point at which it's just getting started.

● ● ●

Why don't we eat each other? I ask the audience. What greater love can you demonstrate to your loved ones when you die than to feed them for a week or two. "Hey, Scott. Come on over tomorrow. We're barbecuing Aunt Mary's leg. No, not the one with the varicose veins, the one that she used to kick her husband around with. We had her liver last night. Man, was it tasty with caramelized onions! Must've been all that Jack Daniel's she used to drink. She's been marinating her liver for thirty years, probably thinking of us all along. What a sweetheart. And Uncle Dave's lungs! Wow, after a lifetime of smoking two packs of unfiltered Camels every day they were just delicious. They don't make smoked bacon like that any more."

Does it say anywhere in the Bible, or the Koran, or the Torah, or the Pali Cannon, or the Brahma Sutra, or the Constitution of the United States of America that you shouldn't eat dead relatives? I don't think so. Sure, if they're diseased they might need some careful handling or radiation or some such, but all that good meat is going to waste. And, as usual, we Americans are wasting more than anyone. What an irony. Fat Americans are dying all over the place of being fat and what do we do? We just throw 'em away! People are under-nourished all over the world and we just trash fine flesh.

● ● ●

I read the papers as I eat because I have to keep up with current affairs so that I can keep my material fresh. But I'd read them anyway because I'm a news junkie. Truth is stranger than fiction - just read the papers and look for those little, incidental stories buried at the bottom of inside pages that say so little but mean so much:

- Man falls off ladder while trimming tree with chain saw and cuts off the head of his wife, who was holding the ladder for him, or
- Man faints while watching his wife give birth in hospital, bangs his head in falling and dies instantly, or
- Woman whose husband died when he fainted while watching her give birth is suing hospital for not warning them in advance that watching your wife give birth in a hospital can be fatal.

And no, these aren't made up. I'm not that good. Just read the papers.

● ● ●

Apotemnophilia, I say to the audience. Anyone know what it is? "Having sex with a gorilla", some wise guy calls. "No," I say, aping a laugh, "good try, but no." I read about it in a newspaper, the

Times of London, no less. Apotemnophilia is getting sexual grati-
fication from having one of your limbs amputated. Really. They
laugh. Really, I stress. I pull out a piece of tattered newsprint, any
piece of tattered newsprint will do, and make a show of quoting
from the article that "There are hundreds of recorded cases world-
wide, possibly thousands of unrecorded cases, and perhaps tens
of thousands of potential sufferers, according to experts. "Sufferers?" I say to the audience, shouldn't that be "enjoyers"? Then what
about these unrecorded cases? I say, tapping the clipping. I suppose
that's people who've managed to cut off a limb but nobody has
noticed. Well, you know what the British are like. Prim and proper.
If your best friend came into work one day with a leg missing, you
wouldn't want to say anything. It might be embarrassing for him. I
tap the clipping again. And how do these so-called "experts" come
up with their numbers? Surveys, perhaps? Ask a thousand people
if any of them have thought of cutting a limb off instead of having
a fuck recently and see how many say no, how many say yes, how
many say "Um, that's interesting. I'd never thought of that. Maybe
I'll give it a try", and how many try to change the subject so the re-
searcher won't notice that they've got a bloody stump where a leg
is supposed to be?

Apotemnophilia. Apo-temno-philia. Nice word. Rolls off the
tongue, after a while. But a bit limiting as a hobby really. I guess
you can only get four orgasms in a lifetime. But hey, that's four
more than my girlfriend has ever managed. Maybe I should mention it to her. If she likes the idea perhaps I could arrange to saw off
her leg as I screw her so that we both get something out of it. With
a bit of work I may even be able to lash the saw to my pelvis so I
can service her hands-free. And I suppose apotemnophiliacs don't
always have to go the whole hog, so to speak. I assume they can cut
off a finger or a toe here or there in foreplay. Must be pretty devas-

tating though, when you're sitting there, legless and armless - well, you'd probably be rocking more than sitting - knowing that your sex life is over for good and all. Of course, you could always try doing something with your dick. But I suppose that's just too obvious for the committed apotemnophiliac, and it's hard to be a practicing apotmenophiliac without being pretty damn committed.

Again, this isn't a gag for young audiences (ah, the surprises they have in store!) or for old audiences, who just plain don't like it. That still leaves me a pretty big window to aim at – mid-20s to mid-50s, say – but it's one of those gags that either works really well or bombs really badly, a bit like apotemnophilia itself, I suppose.

• • •

I've finished eating breakfast and I'm on what must be my tenth cup of coffee. I don't really like coffee. The smell of roasting beans is good, but it's all bad news after that. Even the best coffee is sharp, medium coffee is bitter, and bad coffee is plain disgusting. But that doesn't stop me drinking a couple of gallons a day, partly for the caffeine but mainly because it's just something to do with my hands when I'm not smoking or sipping booze.

Despite the number of times that I frequent this diner, they still treat me like a comparative stranger. I can interpret their slight acknowledgement of me as acquaintanceship if I care to, although I could be treated just as familiarly in a place I've never been to before but where the staff are friendly. I like this aloofness and it's why I keep coming back. We have a civil yet impersonal relationship, this diner and me. What more can I ask? I only wish I'd been able to construct more personal relationships like it. My relationships with the opposite sex tend to go from the lovingly personal to the detestingly impersonal in the time it takes me to forget a birthday or glance at another woman, which is pretty damn fast. I thought of becoming gay at one point, on the baseless assumption that another man would be more tolerant of my idiosyncrasies than another woman. But the gay men I've known seem to be just as demanding as women regarding the behavior of their partners, more so if anything.

● ● ●

Gaydom, I say to the audience, has some great things going for it. No unwanted pregnancies and shared clothing (two wardrobes for the price of one), for example. Being gay is almost as good as being an hermaphrodite, and these days it has even got slightly less of a social stigma. Cross-dressing? Now that seems like a real problem. Now you need twice the wardrobe and you can have problems with both sexes, one for being weird and the other for treading on their turf. AC/DC? Now you're trying to get the best of both worlds. Narcissus was probably AC/DC, and as if he didn't have enough problems with that, he loved himself as well! The trouble with sexuality is that although there are ardent heterosexuals on the one hand – I stretch out my right arm - and ardent homosexuals on the other hand – I stretch out my left arm - most of us fit somewhere in between – I drop my head to look at my feet, but the audience probably think I'm looking at where my dick should be, which is fine, then I look up slowly. The majority of people are close enough to one of these extremes – I waggle my hands – so that they clearly know where they stand, but a big minority – I look at my feet/dick again - are in uncertain territory. I raise my head slowly. Let's call it "no-man's land", which ironically turns out to be a great way of describing it, because if you don't make your mind up and turn one way or the other – I swing my head from right to left - that's exactly what you're going to end up being, no man's man, nor no man's woman, nor no woman's man, nor no woman's woman – I drop my head suddenly to look at my feet again. People laugh, I hope.

Gestures don't come naturally to me. My normal posture is a dead-pan face with my arms at my sides. That's probably why I smoke and drink. They give me something to do with my hands and my mouth, otherwise I would appear to be dead. So when I introduce gestures into my act they probably impress the audience. I know they impress me. My body moving is Lazarus rising – unexpected and decidedly spooky.

Laughter is like drunkenness, I tell the audience as the laughs die down. Laughing really is a lot like drinking heavily:

- It makes you feel good.
- If you do it all the time people think you're crazy.
- If you do it while you're driving it can be dangerous.
- If you do it too much you'll pee in your pants.
- People who're not doing it envy people who are.
- If you do it in church you'll probably get thrown out.
- People who never do it hate people who do.
- If you do it on your own people think you're sad.
- If you do it walking down the street people think you're mad.
- If you make a career out of it you're a loser.

• • •

I put down the newspaper and stare out of the window, my fifteenth cup of coffee brushing my lips - the waiter doesn't bother to ask any more, he just tops up my cup every time he's passing, even if it's in my hand at the time. I need to come up with some new material. My mind is a blank sheet of paper. We have a tougher time of it than most creative people. Painters confront blank canvases, but in their less creative moments they can fill in some background and do the foreground later, and if they really get desperate they can always go and paint the fence, or the garden shed, or the lounge, just to keep their hand in. Musicians can practice scales when they don't feel like composing. Sculptors and potters? Well they can go and use their hands to massage something when the muse isn't there, and if they're really desperate they can always go and masturbate, that's creative, at least I think it is. Writers confront blank sheets of paper, but they can just write away and the bland material may still be useful some time – they don't have to prove themselves with every sentence.

But there's no such thing as half a joke. If what I write isn't funny, I usually can't come back later and make it funny. Jokes are like rifle shots – they either hit the mark or they don't, you only get one bullet per target, and if you miss it's worse than if you hadn't pulled the trigger at all. The people in the audience are like a gang of big angry bears – they don't like you much to start with, and if they see that you're firing bullets at them that are missing the mark, they'll get even sorer. Sure, you can build up a swell in the audience so they'll laugh at a not so good joke riding on the back of a good one. But if the swell declines or it wasn't there in the first place, bad gags get to pile up like rotting carcasses and smell worse, and worse, and worse as each cadaver is loaded onto the pile, to such an extent that not even a good gag can get the audience back on your side again – you have to verge on the brilliant to rescue an audience that you've lost.

• • •

I wander around for a while, hoping that walking will give me some ideas. I sit in a park and smoke a couple of cigarettes. I toy with the idea of buying some groceries and actually cooking my-self something tonight rather than buying food to go. But I've got a gig at 11 on the other side of town and I won't be back home until 1 a.m. or so, later if I find someone to drink with, and by that time I either won't be hungry any more or won't want to unwrap packages, let alone cook, so I let the shopping idea drift out of my mind. I must've eaten food from the majority of restaurants in town, the good ones when someone else is paying, the average ones when my bank balance is holding its own, and the others the rest of the time, which is most of the time. I don't like sitting alone in restaurants in the early hours of the morning at the best of times, and when the state banned smoking in just about every goddam public place that was the last straw. So now I just buy food to take home where I can eat it in my own polluted environment.

A drunk staggers towards me. He's white, 40-ish, filthy, but you can see that there's a good-looking guy lurking under the grime, and his eyes, although they're glazed over for now, look like they could be the front-men for some pretty active intelligence. If I was a street drunk like him, and I easily could be, I'd be lower down the pecking order. This guy is probably an Alpha drunk.

"Hey man," he says.

"Hey," say I.

"How ya doin' there?" he asks, jovially, as if we're old pals, and we probably could be, given time and a bunch of shared beers. He's a conversational drunk. Most of them get to the point pretty quickly, but this guy is more sophisticated. He'll have a sob-story for me. I'm happy to hear it. He may give me some ideas for gags.

"I'm doing fine," I tell him, "how about yourself?"

"Well, funny you should ask me that," he says, as if confiding in me. He sits himself down on the bench beside me and turns his whole torso towards me, one hand gripping the back of the bench and one the seat part, as if he's hanging on, hoping not to get bucked off. His face comes close to mine and his breath washes over me. It's not unpleasant. It sure as hell isn't pleasant either, but I make a point of not reacting. I want to set myself apart in this man's eyes so that he'll remember me. "Today I met a man who didn't run away or tell me to screw off," he'll think to himself.

"It's real funny you should ask me that," he says again, in a conspiratorial whisper this time. I wait for him to press a finger to his lips to confirm the need for secrecy, but he doesn't, and I'm glad to see that he's not that much of a ham.

"To be honest, my man," he says, "I find myself in something of a predicament right now." He stops, his eyes urging me to urge him to go on. I just smile at him, affably I hope, although it appears to me that my smile has a sort of sly, reptilian quality when I catch a glimpse of it in a mirror or see it plastered on my frozen face in a photograph. I'm normally drunk when I'm smiling (well, I'm normally drunk, period) so doing it stone cold sober feels odd, unnatural, a lot like how I feel when I have to do my routine for a lunchtime crowd, at a wedding or something. My act is a thing of the night, so is my smile, so is my metabolism.

He returns my smile with a blank stare. I wonder if his brain has gone to sleep, but suddenly a light flashes in his eyes and he says "Wassyername?" The sudden utterance seems to surprise him as much as it does me because his face momentarily wears a shocked look before he eventually smiles and says "I'm Ben, pleased to meet you," and he takes one of the hands that has been anchoring him to the bench and thrusts it towards me.

His smile is broad and confirms my first impression that he is a handsome man. His skin is brown and stretched tight across his face, the cheekbones in particular, but it's thoroughly dirty. His clothes are good quality but are old and shabby - he's probably been wearing them 24 hours a day for weeks. His hair is plentiful, a light brown with distinguished flashes of grey, but it's ill-kempt, greasy, and matted in parts. His chin is nicely squared, but un-shaven, way beyond the point at which it could be mistaken for designer stubble. He seems to be slim, but I would guess that he's really just skin and bone, with a few globs of fat where the empty calories from the booze have established themselves in order to keep him going between binges. I take his hand in mine as soon as it's offered. No reticence. I want to be his pal, although I have no intention of making him my pal.

"I'm Steve," I say, and he slaps my shoulder with his other hand. We're bosom buddies already.

"You see, it's like this ..." he pauses. He's forgotten my name already. But he manages to dredge it up from the live brain cells that are slowly but surely being outnumbered by dead ones, and eventually, when the live ones are completely surrounded by the dead ones and can't find any other live ones to connect to, he'll be gone. He'll be one of those spaced-out loonies who stand at the side of the street performing their little rituals, one step forward, one step back, endlessly repeated, talking to themselves (and their demons), and randomly shouting at the heavens or passers by, real or imaginary. I know about this, you see, because it's on my career path.

"It's like this ... Steve. I'm a businessman."

I struggle to suppress a laugh, and in doing so I cough, and because our faces are so close (his choice, not mine), he takes the full blast of the cough and, get this, he recoils from me. But he overcomes his disgust and we're back to our face to face conversation in a few seconds.

"I'm a businessman from south of here. From Santa ... Santa ..."

"Santa Claus?" I interject.

"Santa Claus?" he repeats, baffled, then he gets it. "Santa Claus! Ha! That's funny. No, Santa Cruz, I'm from Santa Cruz. Santa Claus! That's funny. You're a comedian, Steve."

"Yes, I am a comedian actually," I say, but he's not interested. This is all about him.

"Anyway, I'm up here on business, and some fucker breaks into my hotel room when I'm out, when I'm out ... when I'm out on ..."

"On business?"

"Yeah, on business, that's right, Steve." He has trouble keeping up a train of thought. But I'll help him with that. I mean, what else are friends for?

"Yeah," he continues, "I'm out on business and some scumbag breaks into my hotel room." He falls silent and his eyes, which have been sparkling for a while, glaze over. "Anyway," he continues after a pause, "the cocksucker steals everything I own. Get it?"

"I think so," I say. "Three people; a fucker, a scumbag and a cocksucker break into your hotel room."

"Eh?"

"The fucker keeps watch while the scumbag breaks down the door and the cocksucker makes off with your possessions, right? Happens all the time. They work in gangs, fuckers, scumbags and cocksuckers. The cops call them FSC gangs."

He looks at me blankly for a while, then he smiles and pats me on the arm.

"Stan ..."

"Steve, " I correct him.

"Steve, you really are a comedian, aren't you?"

"Yes," I tell him, "I really am."

We laugh together, and the bond between us tightens. Maybe he will be my buddy after all.

"So, Steve, the fact of the matter is that I don't have a penny to my name."

"Did you call the cops?"

"Yep. I called the cops, and they told me to fuck off."

"Did you call home?"

"What home?"

"Your home in Santa Cruz?"

"What home in Santa Cruz?"

"Sorry," I say, "you told me you were a businessman from Santa Cruz, and I stupidly leapt to the conclusion that you also had a home there, whereas you obviously just work in Santa Cruz and have a home elsewhere. Did you call home, wherever that is?"

"No, I mean yes, you're right, I do live in Santa Cruz, but I live alone. My girlfriend fucked off a few months ago with some drug dealer who grows meth in the Santa Cruz mountains."

"I didn't know you grew meth. I thought it was manufactured. Are there meth trees in the Santa Cruz mountains?"

"Steve, you know what?"

"Yes."

"What?" he asks with a baffled look, as if wondering how he got to be asking a question.

"You really like me. I'm a comedian."

This reduces him to a fit of laughter. He gasps his words as he laughs "Yes, Steve, that's exactly what I was going to say. I really do like you. You really are a comedian."

"Yes, I really, really am," I tell him. I wish all my audiences were this easy.

"What about your wallet?" I ask him, not wanting to bring a premature end to his mirth, but keen to sort out the details. He needs to work on his story to make it more convincing if he's going to make a living out of this, and I'll try and help him – stories are my specialty, my life is one, a bad one with no punch line that I've yet managed to uncover.

"What about it?" he says, eying me suspiciously.

"Surely, when you were out doing business, when your room

was broken into, you had your wallet with you."

"Ah, that's a good point, Stan."

"Steve."

"Yeah, St..st..steve, good point." He blinks hard, swallows harder, pinches his nose and grimaces. His body seems to be performing its own play in the background, probably trying to find any way it can to yell at him, "Lay off the fucking booze, you idiot!", but he just ignores it and carries on, taking all the tics and spasms as they come.

"You see, Steve, I'd just nipped out to buy a packet of cigarettes, so I hadn't taken my wallet with me. I'd just taken a few bills, enough to buy the cigarettes. All I had on me was the clothes I'm dressed in now, a few bills and the hotel room key. When I came back everything was gone. I mean everything! So all I've got left is what you're looking at." He spreads his arms to illustrate the totality of what was left, is left, then he decides to enhance the impression of nakedness by standing up to show that there were no stashes of bounty sequestered about his body.

A thin man, standing, his arms thrown out at his sides, a pained expression on his face, is bound to evoke images of Christ in one brought up as a Christian, and so it is with me, but not having a cross to support him, and being comprehensively doused in alcohol, Ben breaks the spell by staggering round in a circle and eventually falling back onto the bench, where he once more anchors himself with his two hands, one on the back of the bench, one on the seat. For the committed drunk the world is a bucking bronco of a beast that constantly needs to be subdued. Subduing the world probably gives drunks with A-type personalities their sense of achievement and wholeness.

"What about the bag?" I ask.

"What bag?"

"The bag you've got with you," I say, pointing to a plastic bag that he'd been carrying when he first joined me, and has been sitting in isolation on the far end of the bench ever since his arrival.

"Oh, just a few necessities I managed to scrape up," he says, but from his expression I gather that he doesn't seem to keen to dwell on the subject so, being a pal, I change it for him.

"When did this happen?"

"Yesdy."

"Yesterday?"

"Yes. Yesdy."

This isn't plausible. Not that I have the vaguest intention of believing his story anyway – I am hear to listen and sympathize, not believe - but if I had been inclined to believe it, it would have stretched my credulity beyond any reasonable boundary. It's hard work to get into the sort of state that Ben is in, it's the work of many "yesdys".

We chat for a while longer. Ben is thinking, I assume, that the more we speak the more I will believe him and the more money I will shell out to rescue him from his unfortunate plight as a robbed businessman from Santa Cruz. I am thinking that I'm not getting any useful material out of this encounter, and it is just a matter of listening a bit longer and then giving him a few dollars to help him continue in his vocation as a Master drunk.

"Wanna drink?" he asks, just as I was thinking of moving on.

"A drink?"

"Yes," he says, carefully maneuvering himself to the far end of the bench, never letting go of it, retrieving the plastic bag and then sliding it and himself back towards me. He opens it to reveal a couple of cans of beer and several bottles.

"I have beer, bourbon, vodka, tequila and ..." he holds up a Coke bottle, "and some other stuff in this bottle, and I can't remember what they call it but it makes you feel a damn sight better than Coke-a-fucking-Cola."

Stay with it I say to myself, and I tell Ben that I appreciate his generosity, given his predicament, and I gratefully accept a beer. I decide not to pursue the subject that the purchase value of the booze in the bag is way more than enough to pay for a bus ticket to Santa Cruz.

• • •

It's amazing how smoothly and quickly time passes when you're out in the fresh air having a few drinks and a few cigarettes, chatting to a new-found buddy. We finish the booze in Ben's bag, which mainly consists of finishing off nearly-empty bottles. He drinks most of it, but I have a good enough share, although I politely decline his several offers to partake of the mysterious liquid in the Coke bottle, which, I assume, has been rescued from a dreary life of polishing furniture and has been elevated to the giddy heights of a consciousness-altering substance, and, as a side-effect, an efficient destroyer of the optic nerves, but that's a mere quibble on my part.

Every time Ben takes a sip from the Coke bottle – and he sips rather than swigs in acknowledgement, I presume, of its rare vintage – he winces, puckers his lips, blinks once or twice, swallows hard, shudders, and stamps one or both feet. He then shakes his head slowly to and fro, as if the effort involved in shaking his cranium is significant in such circumstances, or perhaps it is in deference to the slowly decaying organ that resides inside his skull, and a tacit apology for the damage that he is doing to it in the laudable pursuance of the objective of having a good time (aka mental obliteration). It must be good stuff.

I go off to buy more booze and more cigarettes at one point, only to find on returning that Ben has found a new friend, a shapely young Hispanic girl seated on a nearby bench who has probably come into the park to enjoy an undisturbed break. I feel slighted, but the new friend soon tells Ben in very precisely enunciated language to, "Fuck off away from me, you disgusting person" – the Californians manage to be politically correct even when insulting someone. My Ben comes back to me unabashed, swaggering some-what, as if taking pride in even being a failed Ladies' Man, and he continues a story regarding his ex-wife that was interrupted when we ran out of alcohol.

As it starts to grow dark, Ben's mood becomes melancholy.

"I suppose you're wondering how I got to be like this?" he asks, gesturing with his hands to the "this" that he has got to be.

"Actually," I say, "I'm more interested in what you were like before."

He gives me a surprised look.

"Before?" he says. I wonder if he can remember. He probably has a nice, neat, packaged explanation as to why he's a drunk. A smooth, palatable story that makes him appear to be a sad victim of the world's dark forces, worthy of help, hard done by, a deserv-ing recipient of financial aid. A story of a lost job, a deserting wife, a dead child, a crime, a sin, a war, an illness, a vice, an overindul-gence in booze, betting, drugs or sex. We may get around to that later. What I want to know is what he left behind.

He doesn't bother to persist with the fiction that he is an unfor-tunate, stranded businessman from Santa Cruz. He never admits it has been a lie, he just starts telling another story, one that resonates more truthfully with the man I see in front of me, although this too could be a complete fabrication for all I know.

For his ex-wife he paints the picture of a beautiful and loving woman, who for the most part, heroically put up with Ben's many flagrant infidelities, until the day she came home to find Ben up-

stairs in the bedroom simultaneously giving pleasure to two large-breasted teenage girls, while his infant children played unsupervised in the family room below.

"I was a complete shitbag, I admit it. I let down my wife, my family, my parents, my friends, my relations, my colleagues ..." I'll make an editorial interdiction here and cut short his list because it goes on for a long time. "I let everyone down just because I was so damn selfish. It was all about me. I wanted what I wanted, and fuck what anyone else wanted or what my wants meant for them. If I wanted to screw some woman, I screwed her, regardless of what anyone else thought. If it was my best friend's wife or my boss's daughter, well, so what? If I wanted to screw her that's what I did. Fuck the consequences. Now," he said, pausing and sweeping his arm to indicate the park in which we sit, "these are the fucking consequences. This park is my fucking life, this or another one like it, this and the booze, and whatever else I can get hold of to take my mind off all I've lost through my selfishness."

Ben hangs his head. I could tell him that he's still being selfish, sitting here gratifying himself with alcohol, annoying other people, ignoring normal standards of hygiene, running away from his commitments. What he construes as the result of his selfishness is actually the consummation of his selfishness. But I'm not here to discipline, I'm here to listen, to absorb, and not just absorb alcohol, which I'm doing prodigiously, but to absorb Ben, to absorb being Ben and thinking like Ben and feeling like Ben, and although I started it as an experiment in getting some fresh material, now it's more than that. The idea of being Ben is intriguing me.

• • •

Sex is a continuum, I remind the audience, returning to an earlier theme. From plodding heterosexual to prancing homosexual with

all shades of grey in between. But for those people in the middle of the spectrum, those who are struggling to understand their sexuality and place themselves comfortably on the complex map of the sexual landscape, let me tell you that help is at hand. I raise my arms and gaze towards the heavens, which for me is the cobweb-festooned upper area of a nightclub's roof space above the lighting gantry. Help is at hand, brothers and sisters, and brothers or sisters, and sisters or brothers, and brothers who dress up as sisters, and sisters who want to be endowed as their brothers, and vice versa and vice is versa, etc. Hallelujah! Help is at hand. For it was revealed to me in a vision that the key to determining your sexuality is - long pause - curtains. Pause.

Yes, common or garden household drapes give us divine insight into our innermost sexual nature. For I say unto thee, it is impossible for a beer swilling, Mustang driving, football watching, chick shagging, hairy backed heterosexual to hold a conversation of more than two seconds duration on the subject of curtains. Verily I say unto you that the same guy who can wax lyrical on the subject of baseball caps manages to spill the entire contents of his cerebral cortex that pertains to curtains in less than one second, then it takes another second to realize that he has nothing more to say (more in the case of residents of Alabama, Arkansas and North Dakota, where the silence can go on for minutes, or even days) before he changes the subject back to something vastly more interesting, such as the grade of oil to put in his monster truck before embarking on his elk hunting trip to Montana.

Women on the other hand, heterosexual women who love the color pink, chocolate-coated anything, frilly-edged everything, dancing, shopping, candles, and who adore beer swilling, Mustang driving, football watching, chick shagging, hairy backed males, these women can talk for eons on the subject of curtains. In fact

scientists have measured such specimens talking for several days without pause simply on the subject of curtain rings.

So there you have it. A God-given means of determining sexuality. Pause. But, like everything else that God has given us, there are some enigmatic areas. Enigmas really are God's specialty, aren't they? For example, men who can talk about blinds are verging upon the danger area. Real men prefer blondes, not blinds. As to women who prefer blinds to curtains, I advise that men considering relationships with such persons should check the chick's wardrobes and CD collections before making commitments, being especially watchful for dungarees, chewing tobacco and Dusty Springfield albums.

• • •

"So what do you do for a living, Steve?" Ben asks at last. We've been talking for almost three hours exclusively about Ben. Well, actually I've done very little of the talking, and what I have done has been solely to encourage Ben to talk more about Ben, which he's very happy to do.

"I'm a comedian."

"Ha! No, come on, really, what do you do?"

"I'm a comic, a stand-up comic."

He looks at me blankly. I guess he's trying to equate this passive, expressionless, humorless individual, who hasn't told a joke all afternoon, to a guy who makes people laugh for a living. I need his mind to take a quantum leap, to ignore what his senses are telling him intuitively, and believe what I've just told him verbally. It's a common reaction and one that, I assume, comics throughout the ages have learned to accept. When they're not on the stage, most comedians are not in the slightest bit funny. It's the price we pay for bringing laughter to others – we share none of it ourselves.

"Really?" he says, reaching for the Coke bottle and its noxious contents, obviously needing access to a new level of perception in order to assimilate this shocking information. I could have told him I did anything for a living – politician, racing driver, pornographer, shopkeeper, computer programmer, cop, Wal*Mart greeter, groupie - and he probably would have accepted it without blinking, and he's now blinking madly, but I presume that's a consequence of the Coke bottle swig, and not of the news that I've just imparted.

"Yes, really. I'm doing a gig tonight as it happens. Want to come?"

"Me? No, I mean … well, I'm kinda busy. Not that I wouldn't like to but ... you see, I … well ... I have something else arranged, like … like ..."

"Like sitting in this park and getting more drunk?" I ask. It's the first contentious thing I've said since we met, and it may even be the longest sentence I've uttered or had the chance to utter. I pat him on the arm to show that I mean it as a friendly enjoinder and not as a hostile challenge.

"Come on Ben. I'll take you there in a taxi, buy you a few drinks. You listen to my performance then we have a few more drinks, get something to eat, maybe, then have a few more drinks and come back here. How's that?"

"You think ... you think …" I expect he's going to say "You think I'm crazy," but instead he says, "You think they'll let me in?"

I laugh, in relief as much as anything. It matters what this drunk thinks of me - that's about as accurate a measure of my self-confidence as you can get.

• • •

I can't even begin to count the number of nights I've had that end with a sour taste in my mouth from booze and cigarettes, a

headache, indigestion, and a reconfirmation of the self-knowledge that my life is going nowhere. I sometimes believe that, despite laughing, the audience hasn't really found my jokes funny, and they've shown appreciation just to humor me, the audience amusing the comic. And those are the good nights. But every now and again, after a particularly good set, a few people will come and see me afterwards to say hello, to thank me, to congratulate me perhaps, to tell me that they have some material that they would like me to look at (heaven forbid), to buy me a drink (heaven be praised), or even (quaintest of all) to ask for my autograph - I see them printing my name and a descriptive phrase underneath to remind them who the hell I am, just in case I become famous one of these days. "Don't bother", I want to say to them, "you're wasting ink and paper and finger muscle".

Every now and again a woman will come up to me afterwards with a glint in her eye, and once a year, or once a decade, or once in a blue moon, she will be attractive and we'll get to shoot the breeze. But I know the point will come when she'll make up an excuse – I'm meeting my friends, or, my husband is waiting for me in the bar, or, my girlfriend is waiting for me in a lesbian nightclub, or something else to show that our meeting is irretrievably over – and she'll leave, disappointed at the off-stage reality. Leaving me to my fuck-awful self.

I understand. The me on the stage is in control. I'm running things. I'm constructing the images, setting the scene, creating the situations, laying down the rules. And in that setting I can be funny because I define what is funny. But once I'm off the stage the world pokes its nose in and I'm no longer in control, and when that happens I'm not funny any more. I'm just … me, and me isn't funny. At all.

• • •

After a full more pulls on the Coke bottle, Ben agrees to come and watch my performance. I can't say that he appears to be happy about the prospect of the evening that I've planned for him, which is a little surprising. In fact, his lack of zeal is somewhat disappointing, but I'm trying to keep myself out of it. Ben surely has his own routine, his rut, and to him my life must look like pure chaos, even when compared to the squalid backdrop against which he lives his own.

"Where do you get your jokes from?" Ben asks. I tell him that I make them up. He asks me to tell him one, probably expecting a ticklish one-liner. I tell him that I do comic monologues rather than jokes. He looks a bit disappointed (he is, after all, a man whose life is about quick hits) but he still wants to hear one. I give him the "apotemnophilia" shtick, on the prejudiced assumption that a depraved guy will relate to a depraved practice. But he gets hung up on the word apotemnophilia, and won't let me go on with the joke until I've spelt it out time after time so that he can memorize it and pronounce it himself. All this takes about five minutes, and by that time I'm about ready to give up and tell him a one-liner about Roman Catholic priests and vacuum cleaners instead. Anyway, we get through it eventually, and when he gets the hang of it, when he understands that he has to think a bit to get the gags and they won't just bang him on the nose like a mother-in-law joke, then he actually gets amused.

And I can tell when people are really amused and not just pretending to be. Their faces are somehow different, their eyes retreat, as if they're looking inside their skulls to watch over a bit of private joy. That's when humor is like a drug, an outside influence resonating somehow with your brain and making it feel different to the extent that it can make your mouth spring open, your stomach muscles go into a spasm, and repetitive barks of sound hammer out of your mouth. And it makes you feel good, which is what it all comes down to, what we're all aiming at. In Ben's case the addiction to feeling good has overtaken his whole life, but the medium he's using to get there is destroying his whole life.

● ● ●

Candles, I tell the audience, now there's another gender-dividing subject, not quite as clearly delineated between the sexes as curtains, probably because men like fire, but you don't see a whole lot of men in candle shops, not on their own.

Women like candles, no, they love candles. Romantic evenings have to have candles. A woman on one side of the table, a man on the other. I can't say for sure what the woman is thinking about, but I damn well know what the man is thinking about, and when he's not peeping down the woman's cleavage he's confronted by the most blatant phallic symbol you can imagine, a great big candle.

"Come on," the woman is saying, via her candle, "I'm expecting something as big and straight and erect as this firm and silky-smooth column of fire." She's issuing a challenge. "If you can't match this," she's saying, "I'll just go to bed with a candle instead, and if I snuff it out beforehand it won't dribble all over me."

Have you seen women in candle shops? They pick them up, they feel them, they rub their fingers up and down them, they fiddle coyly with the wick, they sniff them. I'm surprised that candle shops don't have fitting rooms out back.

● ● ●

"I've always been addicted to something," Ben tells me. When he was a kid he had a succession of obsessive hobbies. Baseball cards, toy trains, pet mice, postage stamps, model airplanes, basketball, one after the other, and every one completely overtook him. If it was pet mice that he was into, then he lived and breathed mice. Everything he read, bought, thought, did had to do with mice; they weren't just the most important thing to him, they were the only thing to him. Until the next thing. Then he'd drop one fad like a hot potato and move on to the next, completely immersing himself in it and not having the faintest idea why he'd found the last fad so goddam wonderful when the current one was the only thing in the world worth thinking about. I pity his parents having to clean up one neglected mania after another.

But all this was relatively harmless, weird, but harmless. He was late getting around to the subject of girls because his motorcycle craze took a hold of him when he was sixteen and didn't loosen its grip until he was nineteen. But when it did, the subject of sex was there to fill the void, and fill the fucking void it did. Ben became a slave to sex, a shag junkie, a professional pervert, and he got seedily stuck in that obsession until he was 23 when he was "rescued" by the woman who became his wife, to whom he swore love and devotion, but as far as I can tell she was really just the next obsession.

The wife fad lasted long enough for them to start a family, but the sex mania wasn't taking defeat lying down, and, sure enough, when the subtle titillation of marriage and family life let its defenses drop, the unsubtle sex fad rushed back to center-stage, grabbed his penis and dragged him once more to the world of debauchery that blew his family apart.

He gives me graphic accounts of his sex life, and it's such a sordid tale he tells that I can't imagine he's making it up. When sex and multiple perversions on the theme started to have less appeal, booze and drugs were there to spice things up, and soon the booze and drugs were as important as the sex, and then they became more important than the sex. So there he was, seamlessly transported into his next fad, the one he's now in, the one that's killing him. The way out of Ben's current predicament is simple. It's the way into his next one. He has to find a new obsession, one that's slightly less poisonous.

• • •

I don't get this big thing about being faithful, I tell the audience. If I love my wife, if I do all the right husbandly things, if I never forget anniversaries and birthdays, if I'm always there for my children, if I buy her surprise treats every now and again, if I ensure that we have our fair measure of romantic moments, if I'm a satisfying and considerate lover, if I share the housework, if I frequently give her affectionate, non-sexual cuddles to show that I love her apart from the sexual component, and if I generally play the role of a really good mate, what does it matter if I go and stick my cock in another woman now and again, a woman for whom I never do most of the things that I do for my wife? My wife gets a huge superset of the things that the other woman gets – the other woman gets the cock sticking and not much else. In fact, my wife doesn't even have to put up with much cock sticking any more, whereas that's not an option for the other woman, whose primary role, whose raison d'etre is to be cock stuck.

The problem is that word, "unfaithful". That's a loaded word. Let's just be literal and call it a random act of cock sticking, as compared to cock sticking by a social contract, namely marriage. I can look at other women, smile at them, shake hands with them, hug them, send them emails, take them to lunch, tell them dirty jokes, or clean ones. I can even like them more than my wife, that's no sin. But as soon as you stick the old cock in there you're suddenly evil. Isn't that putting the cart before the horse? The carnal before the emotional?

People talk about respect. What's respect got to do with it? I can respect you and steal your wallet. I can respect you and think you're fat. I can respect you and fuck your wife and continue to respect you and your wife and my wife. It's just cock sticking, that's all.

• • •

"What makes things funny? What makes people laugh?" Ben asks me. Do I pause? Do I scratch my head? Do I ruminate? Do I guffaw and say wisely, "Oh Ben, if only I knew?" No, of course I don't. I know perfectly well what makes people laugh. Laughter is caused by tricking the brain. When the brain sees two scenarios, one slightly different from the other, but only slightly different, it releases a chemical that sets off a chain reaction that causes laughter. In other words, humor comes out of a normal situation and twisting it slightly so that the two scenarios, the normal one and the twisted one, are seen juxtaposed. Here's an example in terms of a very basic gag. It's not a very funny gag, but it's simple, so it illustrates the point without overlaying it with unnecessary levels of complexity.

A man goes to the doctor. The doctor says, "What's the problem?" The man says, "Doctor, I've got hemorrhoids." The doctor doesn't reply immediately. He sits there. He mops his brow. He scratches his chin. He taps the desk looking pensive. All the while, the patient is writhing on the chair because that's what you do when you've got hemorrhoids. Then the doctor gets up, goes to the corner of his office and retrieves a long pole with a hook on the end. The patient panics. "Doctor!" he yells, "What are you going to do to me?!" "It's alright, says the doctor, "I'm just going to open the windows."

As I said, a simple joke, a crude joke, just one step up the ladder from lavatory humor, or maybe not even that elevated. A prosaic subject. Actually a painfully mundane subject for a middle-aged man like me, who eats a diet that almost exclusively exists of roughage-free, fried food. But the point is that a simple scene is set (a visit to the doctor), an unexpected twist introduced (the pole), then the divergent views of the doctor (opening the window to let in some air) and the patient (contemplating having a gaff stuck three feet up his ass) give the two scenes that are presented to the brain, which reacts accordingly, and laughter ensues.

If the two scenes that are presented to the brain are too far out of whack, the humor becomes either too obvious (slapstick comedy), or too profound (absurdist comedy), neither of which are to my taste. I hate practical jokes, for example, which are the layman's incarnation of slapstick, and, as a professional, I hate jokes that require a lot of thought – thinking about laughing is as ludicrous as performing open-heart surgery on yourself.

•••

We go to the club. It's a place called "Digger's" run by two tall, blonde Australians, one male the other not, at least not quite. I do my act. I'm drunk, but the audience is more drunk, so it goes okay. I can always rely on Australians to be more drunk than I am. Ben's at a table right next to the stage. I've set him up with a full bottle of brandy, but his closely guarded bag of hooch is carefully stashed under his chair, and I notice him dipping into it now and again to get some fortification from the contents of the Coke bottle, which must make the brandy taste like a flimsy-limbed, fluffily-bearded adolescent.

Ben has a raucous laugh, and with every visit of the Coke bottle to his lips the laugh becomes more raucous. He often leads the laughter so he turns out to be a real asset for a while, given that this is an audience intent on laughter – they'd be screaming there heads off if I was reading passages from the Bible, dull passages about who begat whom from whose loins. Audiences like this offer no challenge, not that I'm looking for challenges, but I like to have a vague suspicion that I'm earning my money, and I have none of that feeling tonight.

It gets to near the end of my set and Ben laughs so hard at the candle gag that he falls off his chair. He sprawls around for a while before a couple of people lift him up and plonk him back in his seat. There's a geeky guy in the audience who's been staring at me fixedly since I came on stage – I know the sort, he's probably writing a book on the theory of comedy and he'll come up to me later and ask me who my influences are ("Jack Daniels, and Colonel Sanders," I'll tell him). Apart from this one nerd, the whole goddam audience is watching Ben, who jumps to his feet and shouts, "Sorry folks! I'm legless. Blame it on the apotemnophilia." The drunken rabble that constitute 99% of the audience (i.e. everyone minus the geek) finds this fucking hilarious, and I'm just standing on the stage, like a lemon, completely irrelevant.

Now Ben's in the limelight he's loving it, and the fucked up, antipodean audience are loving it too. He gives a brief introduction to the subject of apotemnophilia, the Reader's Digest version, and I have to say it's not bad, it almost makes me chuckle, and that's not a trivial accomplishment.

"I'd give my right arm to have an orgasm," he shouts. "In fact, I already have!" And he pulls his hand up into his jacket sleeve and lets his arm hang loose so he looks like an amputee. Laughter ensues, more laughter than any of my gags provoked, and I thought I was doing pretty well.

"My buddy Stan," he shouts, pointing at me. "Steve!" I shout back, but nobody hears me – I can barely hear myself. "My buddy Stan," he continues, "asked me to give him a hand tonight." He pauses then grins and wags his finger at me in mock admonishment. "I know what you've been up to, Stan," he says, and that just about brings the fucking booze-soaked house down.

"Talking of apotemnophilia," Ben goes on, pronouncing the word as if he's been using it all his life, "do you know what they call a man with no arms and no legs in a swimming pool?" Short pause. "Bob!" he yells, and after the second that it takes alcohol ravaged synapses to connect, a scream of hysterical laughter overtakes the audience. I walk off the stage.

• • •

Two hours later and we're back on the bench in the park. Ben is ecstatic.

"I really think I can make this work, Stan." I don't bother to correct him. I don't care. I'll change my name to Stan if that helps.

"I just love making people laugh," he says, his eyes bright. He's a different man to the one I met here 12 hours ago.

He has good timing, I admit, and so what if he is recycling other people's material? There's many a good comic who's made a living out of doing that.

I pull the Coke bottle out of the bag and offer it to him. He declines.

"I just know I can make this work," he says, and I believe him because I know that he'll apply the same intensity to being a comic as he did to breeding mice, and collecting stamps, and to basketball, and to motorcycles, and to sex. He'll apply more effort in a week than I've applied in a lifetime.

I sip from the Coke bottle. I wince, blink, shudder and stamp one foot on the ground, or maybe both. I'll get the hang of it, and so will Ben. •

Part 2 - Life with others

The smell in the bathroom

I had been taught how fast light travels, and I had been taught how fast sound travels, but I had no idea how fast a smell traveled. Not until that day. I still don't know the precise speed, but I know that in the case of Jim, and in the case of that house, the odor was in the kitchen within three seconds of the bathroom door swinging back.

We all make a smell in the bathroom from time to time. For you it may be infrequent and mild, or, at the other extreme, it may be regular and repulsive. Then again, in very rare cases you may be like my past room-mate Jim, which means to say that you're way off the Richter Scale of bathroom odors. Out there. In another league. Something else. So far out of the ordinary that the vile becomes fascinating but remains vile.

I was sharing a house with three men and a girl. One of the men left so we advertised the vacancy. We thought we were best described as "young professionals", so in the ad that's how we defined the person who would probably best fit in with us. Naturally, if the men were honest, we would have advertised for a beautiful nymphomaniac and made no mention of professional standing. But we allowed our newly burgeoning adult natures to prevail and left the precise wording to the female of the group, Sally, who was younger than either of we men but had more maturity than the two of us combined times ten.

Many people called, and many said they would drop by. But they didn't, which puzzled us, then worried us. Out of the blue, Jim appeared on the doorstep. Nice looking guy. Friendly. Greg (who reads a lot) described him as "rakishly handsome" – I don't know exactly what he read to come up with that sort of Victorian-era description, but Sally knowingly said she agreed, so I agreed also, both to the description and to having him join us.

Things were fine for precisely 18 hours. Those were the hours between Jim turning up with his things at 2 p.m. on Saturday, and him exiting the bathroom at 10 a.m. the next day. I remember that first emergence from the bathroom and what I was doing in the same way I remember where I was when I heard that John Lennon had been murdered.

• • •

Sally, Greg and I were all drinking coffee in the kitchen, which was close to Jim's bathroom. In honor of our new roommate, Sally was making eggs, bacon and pancakes, and we were enjoying the cooking smells over freshly brewed coffee when Jim's bathroom door swung back. Sally was the first to notice, but no sooner had she started to communicate a warning with a "What the ..?" than she started gagging and ran from the room with her hand jammed so tightly over her mouth that to this day I can envisage the marks her fingertips made in the flesh of her cheeks. Greg and I looked at each other puzzled, then we looked at our coffee, then at the half-cooked breakfast, then the smell got us both at more or less the same time. For the briefest interval – no more than a few milliseconds – I thought I might be able to grit it out. But that naïve judgment was soon dashed as the immensity of what I was encountering began to register.

I'm a pretty laid-back guy in general. I think before I act, and I like to be seen as cool-headed, so I make an effort to restrain myself from reacting quickly to non-life-threatening situations. But desperate times call for desperate measures, and in this case my legs were calling the shots, as dictated by my olfactory system, which clearly felt itself to be under mortal attack. Almost before I knew it I was out in the back yard, as were a pasty-faced Greg and a still-gagging Sally.

I caught Sally's eye. I don't know if she was suppressing a laugh or vomit. I caught Greg's eye – there was no doubt in his case, and a coffee-colored stream was soon being sprayed over the hardy annuals that edged the lawn.

"Jesus! What was that?" said Sally at last between deep breaths.

"Probably nothing," I said, reverting to the relaxed image that I wanted to project. "Just a one-off. Perhaps he's nervous. New home, new people. It's screwed up his digestive system."

"You think so?" said Sally, her chest still heaving.

"God, I hope so," said Greg, wiping his mouth with the back of his hand.

We all had things to do, so we didn't see much of each other for the rest of the day and didn't get to talk about it any more. I saw Jim in the early afternoon. We had a pleasant chat, I helped him move some furniture around in his room, and the shock of the morning was dispelled from my mind.

But Monday put paid to any sense of complacency I might have been experiencing.

• • •

I was eating a bowl of cereal in the kitchen. I hadn't noticed Jim go into the bathroom. Greg ambled into the kitchen to join me, still in his bathrobe and rubbing his eyes. When the bathroom door opened I don't remember feeling apprehensive, and even when I saw that it was Jim evacuating it I didn't quite put two and two together. But within seconds my nose was ringing a strident alarm bell and my legs were heading for the garden, again.

Too late. The odor overcame me before I could grip the handle of the door leading to the garden, to the wonderful fresh, full of invigorating and life-nourishing outside air. This time it was my turn to gag, and the cereal that had tasted so good on the way down was tasting really bitter on the way up. Greg was right behind me, but having seen my condition he was taking great pains to hold his breath, and was still holding it as he ran past me and headed for the far end of the yard. He stopped at the perimeter fence, turned and breathed, but still with his hands over his mouth.

Greg and I met in the center of the lawn.

"This is no joke," he said, and I was about to reply when Sally burst out of the door and replayed Greg's antics. We then reconvened the impromptu tri-partite meeting that we'd had on Sunday.

"What are we going to do about this?" said Sally.

"Jesus!" said Greg.

"This can't go on," said Sally.

"Jesus!" said Greg.

"Let's be rational about this," I said.

"Je..." said Greg, interrupting himself as he probably realized he was becoming repetitive.

They both looked at me, Sally expectant, Greg cynical. I hadn't given a lot of rational thought to the subject, but now I forced myself.

"There's a ventilator in the bathroom," I said. Sally nodded. Greg blinked.

"He needs to turn it on," I added.

"Will you tell him?" asked Sally, and I couldn't tell if her tone was imploring or suspicious, or both.

"No need," said Greg. Greg was an aspiring attorney by profession, but a handyman by nature. "I can sort out the wiring so that it comes on automatically when he turns on the light."

Sally extended her hands, one for my shoulder, one for Greg's. "Great idea," she said.

"What if he doesn't turn on the light?" I asked. Sally looked at me as if I'd just diagnosed her with brain cancer.

"Are you joking?" said Greg. "That bathroom is like the Black

Hole of Calcutta." Again, I wasn't clear as to the value of the historical allusion from the well-read Greg, but I was happy to see his confidence.

"I'll come back at lunchtime and fix it," said Greg, our hero.

We went back into the house, cautiously, heading straight for our individual rooms. I got ready to leave quickly, very quickly. I estimate that not more than two minutes passed between my coming in from the garden and getting into my car to head for the office. Looking in the rear-view mirror as I drove down the road, I saw Sally jump into her car, and then Greg, still in his bathrobe, dashing towards his Toyota with a bundle of clothes under one arm.

• • •

Tuesday morning. Sally, Greg and I are in the kitchen at 7 a.m. We're all dressed and ready for work, our briefcases at our feet. Greg and I are gulping down our breakfasts. Sally is drinking coffee, saying that she'll pick up something to eat on the way to work, adding, "if I can face it" as a mumble into her coffee cup. We're trying to make conversation, but all our eyes are on the doorway, and beyond it to the door to the bathroom across the corridor.

We hear the door to Jim's room open. We look at each other. We hear the bathroom door close.

"Why the hell don't we shut the kitchen door?" says Sally, after a long silence.

"Because I want to see if it works," says Greg.

"To hell with that," says Sally, grabbing her bag and leaving in the fastest move I've seen her make since a slightly weird ex-boyfriend of hers showed up at the house in a very weird state at 3 a.m. a few months ago.

Greg and I sit, waiting. We hear the extractor fan come on.

"Is it capable of getting rid of that smell?" I ask.

"I don't know," says Greg. "I checked out the vent, and it's fine. If that doesn't work, well ..."

We hear the toilet flush, and soon afterwards we hear the fan turn off and then see the bathroom door open. Ten seconds later we're both out in the yard.

"Better?" asks Greg, somewhat imploringly.

"Slightly," I answer. "Perhaps," I add. We both had the sense to bring our bags with us, and after circling the house at a safe distance we set off for work.

• • •

During the next week we all developed avoidance strategies, tailored to the individual, but based on the common themes of:

1) Rapidly improvised facemasks. I had hoped that the many handkerchiefs given to me every Christmas by various aunts would come in useful for something one day, and this was their day.

2) Prodigious amounts of industrial strength air freshener. Greg had a friend who purchased the stuff in bulk for an airport, and he managed to get a good discount on a quantity purchase.

3) The most effective stratagem of all; being out of the house from the time Jim disappeared into the bathroom on his first visit of the day, until at least two hours after he emerged. One good thing to be said for Jim is that his habits were extremely regular, and once we had survived the morning onslaught, the air was relatively sweet for the next 22 hours or so.

Once the morning Diaspora was over, life went on pretty much as normal. Jim proved to be just as affable and amenable as we had hoped, and he probably thought he was starting to fit in nicely. But there were perturbations that reminded us that we were applying short-term fixes to a long-term problem.

● ● ●

When I drew up at the house one evening, I saw Sally standing on the front lawn. She had bags of groceries in each hand but was staring fixedly at the ground. I got out of my car and joined her.

"What is it?" I asked, but I immediately saw that her attention was focused on a dead bird at her feet. I looked up to the guttering, and beyond it to the edge of the roof, and beyond that to a pipe that marked the outlet from one of the air vents. It was the vent from Jim's bathroom.

"Nothing," Sally replied, unconvincingly. Like a mime show we both looked from the bird, to the vent, to the bird, and back again, then walked silently into the house.

Two days later, a Thursday evening. The phone rings. I answer. "Have you noticed a problem with the drains lately?" asks one of our neighbors.

"A problem with the drains?" I repeat. I'm in the kitchen with Sally.

"Oh, no," says Sally, "now he's poisoning the whole bloody town."

"Yes," says the neighbor. "There's been a bad smell in the air the past couple of days. It made my wife feel sick today."

"Made your wife sick?"

"Christ," says Sally. "First the birdlife, now the human population."

"Yes, and we don't seem to be having a problem ourselves, not with our drains, so I was wondering if anyone else might be having a problem."

"Not that I'm aware of," I say, " but we'll keep watching, or rather, we'll keep sniffing," I add.

The next day, Friday, I've been at work for five minutes when the phone rings. It's Sally. She patches in Greg.

"What are we going to do about this?" she asks. Demands.

"Talk to him," I say.

"Who?" both Sally and Greg ask, simultaneously, impatiently.

"Jim, of course," I say, tetchily.

"No, who's going to talk to him?" asks Sally, equally tetchily. All of our nerves are frayed.

"All of us," I say, trying to be calm, but aware that my voice is up an octave or two.

"Tonight," says Sally. "We'll have dinner together. I'll do the food. You two can do the wine. I'll call him and tell him we're having dinner to discuss house policy or something. We'll flip a coin to decide who's going to raise the subject, but all of us must chip in immediately. Okay?"

We agree.

"But Sally," I say, before we hang up. "Nothing spicy for dinner." Nobody laughs, and I hadn't intended it as a joke anyway.

• • •

To say there was tension in the air as we prepared dinner that evening would be a considerable understatement. All four of us were in and out of the kitchen – Sally, Greg and I noticeably loading up on booze. At one point Jim excused himself to call his girlfriend from his room. Sally produced a coin.

"Heads or tails?" she said to Greg.

"What? Well ... heads, I s-s-suppose," he said, uncharacteristically jamming his fingers into his mouth and chewing at his nails.

She tossed the coin, caught it and exposed a tail in her upturned hand. Coin tossings and callings proceeded for the next few minutes. I lost track of what it all meant, and we were getting so drunk I suspect none of us knew what was really going on. But eventually Sally turned to me and said, "Okay, that's it. Decided. You raise it and we'll support you."

"Yes," added Greg, a little bit too eagerly for my liking.

"But ..." I said, before their intent gazes persuaded me that further debate was pointless, and I might just as well swallow it.

Dinner proceeded. Jim seemed to be more cheerful than ever, patently unaffected by the nervousness that the rest of us were expressing in our every gesture. Sally knocked over a glass of wine. Greg knocked over a bottle of wine. I dropped the pepper mill into the middle of my plate of pasta, splattering (non-spicy) tomato sauce over a radius that defied the laws of physics.

I was drunk, Sally was very drunk, and Greg was practically comatose – he had reached that point where he was unable to focus his eyes and everything received a glazed, empty stare. Jim was tipsy, but the least drunk of any of us by far. Not knowing him very well meant that I was unable to judge if this was a good thing or not. Did he get more mellow or more angry as he drank more? In what state was he more likely to receive the news? With laughter as opposed to violence? Nonchalance as opposed to hysteria?

I was also worrying that having raised the subject, what more was there to say. I mean, what could the poor guy do? His guts stank. What could he do about it? How many homes had he been chased from for this very reason? Did he at last think he'd found a safe refuge? A haven amongst self-proclaimed "professional people", who would be more sympathetic than the uncaring louts who had ejected him from so many places in the past? Or maybe the news would hit him out of the blue? It was hard to imagine, but perhaps the problem had only recently begun, or he had always lived in smell-proofed environments, or amongst people with chronically obstructed nasal passages, or ... I stopped myself thinking. The thinking was making me sober and sober was the last thing I wanted to be.

If the pending announcement hadn't been looming over me, the evening would have been fun. Sally seemed to have forgotten the reason for the dinner altogether and was laughing a lot. She was also sprawling across the table from time to time, giving me a warming glimpse down her blouse at her full, motherly bosom.

Greg was pretty much out of it, but a gormless smile was plastered across his face, so he wasn't dampening the occasion in any way.

As has happened to me a number of times during the course of my life, when I find myself in stressful situations something odd seems to go on in my brain. It's as if the part that has the nasty job to handle detaches itself from the rest of my mind and just gets on with it, like John Wayne saying "to hell with this pussyfooting around" and going and saving the day whilst the rest of the wagon train vacillates timidly. It's as if part of me (the majority) stands back and watches another, braver part (the minority) address the problem.

I'm sure that psychiatrists have a term for it, "protective disassociative ablatory syndrome" or some such – I simply call it "bloody good luck". It happened that night, thank God. Without consciously planning it, I heard myself, the other me, the tiny, brave me saying, "Jim, we have an issue to discuss."

Sally's laugh closed off abruptly and silence engulfed the room as quickly, thoroughly and stiflingly as Jim's smell. Jim didn't reply, but just looked at me, wide-eyed, innocent, vulnerable.

"Jim, the smell when you use the bathroom," the other me said. "Good use of words," the normal me thought. I'm making it sound as if the smell and Jim aren't necessarily connected. As if his bowels are a renegade part of his body, parasitically living off the rest of the Jim organism.

"Uh?" said Jim.

Greg made a noise that could have been a "yes" or maybe it was just a nervous hiccup.

"Sorry Jim," said the reliable Sally. She reached across the table, presumably to grab his arm in a gesture of comfort and conciliation, but her reach fell a few inches short and instead her grasping hand fell into a glop of poached pear in chocolate sauce that remained on Jim's dessert plate. Sally didn't seem to notice, and I could see her fingers gently massaging the piece of pear as if it were Jim's hand.

"Sorry, Jim, but it's true," she continued, but then, unfortunately, added a reflexive "Yuck!", which was the realization of where her hand had landed, although Jim may not have interpreted it that way.

"Jim," said Greg, heroically struggling to enunciate words through a mouth numbed by as much booze as I'd seen him drink in all the time I'd known him put together. "Jim, when you leave the bathroom each morning, each and every morning, it stinks."

"I'm afraid it does," said the normal me, which could now pathetically emerge from it's shell.

"Really stinks," added Greg, unnecessarily.

"Sorry Jim," said Sally, still wiping at her hand with a napkin.

"I mean really stinks!" added Greg, "like nothing has ever stonk … I mean stunk!"

"Greg," said Sally.

"I mean the smell is ..." continued Greg, unstoppably.

"Greg!" said both Sally and I. But Greg needed no more words, his next gesture was a perfectly adequate, albeit dramatic, description of the smell. He threw up over the table, the resulting emission managing to reach into all the dessert remainders.

• • •

The next day, Saturday, we slept in. As far as I could tell, I was the first one up, my head pounding viciously. Jim's bedroom door was shut. The nearby bathroom door was open, but there was no smell. I breathed a sigh of relief and went into the kitchen.

On the table, which was somewhat cleaned up from last night's debauchery, but still not in a particularly wholesome state, was a check with a note sticking to it that read "One week's rent. Sorry it didn't work out."

Jim had packed in the night and left. His bedroom and the bathroom he used were clean, spotlessly clean. The bathroom smelt positively fresh, of lemon – I hated it. •

The crapper a.k.a. The lavatory

Many people think that this crude word for the flush toilet originates from its inventor Thomas Crapper, born in 1856. However, although Thomas was a plumber and sanitary engineer, who holds some patents for water closet inventions, and who supplied Edward VII's Sandringham House in the 1880s, there are others who are credited with its invention. Names such as Sir John Harington (16th century), Alexander Cummings, George Jennings, and Albert Gilbin often come up when researching the topic.

It wasn't until 1859 that the word crap appeared in a dictionary of slang.

Heart and sole

Ilook around at the floor. After just five minutes it's in the same state as at the last three stores after 30 minutes, 20 minutes and 10 minutes respectively. She's getting into her stride.

There are eight pairs of shoes scattered around, which she's in various stages of trying on, rejecting, short-listing or just plain mulling over. And not just shoes. Shoes come out of boxes, and they're packed in other stuff, and yet more stuff is packed in them to make them look good when there are no feet in them. The floor is starting to look like a disorganized taxidermist's workshop.

If I wasn't here I could be out cycling, or at the beach, or watching a movie, or drinking beer with friends as we incinerate dead cow. I could be with other men, talking about women, lying about past conquests and swapping dirty jokes. At this precise moment, talking about women would be infinitely preferable to actually being with one.

"What do you think of this," she says, holding up one shoe, "compared to this," she says, holding up another.

I gaze at the two. One then the other. The other then the one. To and fro. The two allegedly different shoes are thrust at me, as if in challenge to my faculties of differentiation. For the life of me I can't see any difference between them. They're both shiny black. They're the same shape, have the same strap, the same buckle. They even look the same underneath for God's sake!

"They're identical," I say flatly, hoping that the tone of my voice will convey my feelings. I've been working on maintaining an exasperated facial expression and body language (humped shoulders, dragged feet) for the past hour, but it hasn't worked. Perhaps I can get the message across in my tone of voice before I have to take the last resort and tell her outright that I'm bored out of my skull and she's being pernickity beyond belief.

They have robots to vacuum floors these days. We should have robots to accompany women shopping, robots that would say all the right things – "no, you're bottom doesn't look big in that dress" - without even the tiniest hint of a frown or a sigh, robots that could trail after their female mistresses to hundreds of shops in a day, so that even when the woman has collapsed on the sidewalk from exhaustion, the robot would cheerfully say, "Oooh look, there's a shop over there we could try!" With robots like this – dressed in pants and with a permanent inane grin painted on their metallic faces – we men could stay at home doing something infinitely more enjoyable, such as scouring the oven or cleaning window blinds.

"Of course they're not identical," she says, rolling her eyes to show some of the same frustration that I feel. "Look, the strap is different. Can't you see?"

I inspect the two shoes again. There is a very slight difference between the thin straps, but it's almost undetectable. Sherlock Holmes would have been proud to notice the difference without prompting. I look at her, expecting to see some sign of amusement, as if she's joking, playing with me. There is none. From her perspective we're having a serious debate about a nuance of patterning on a few millimeters of leather.

"Look," I say, "you're a reasonably attractive woman." I shouldn't have said "reasonably", and I know it as soon as the word is uttered, but I continue unabashed - backtracking would weaken my position. "Anyone looking at you is going to look at other things before they look at your shoes, and they're never, ever going to look at the fine detail of the straps before they make a judgment."

"What makes you think I'm buying these shoes to affect what people think of me?" Her eyes brighten as she sees one of her favorite discussion subjects – "I wear what I like because I like it, screw everyone else" – looms on the horizon. For her the vista associated with this subject is bright invigorating sunshine; for me it is dark, threatening clouds. I try to use logic, which in this situation is as sensible as using a hand grenade to solve world hunger.

"You told me earlier that you were looking for a pair of practical, comfortable shoes. If you're buying shoes for functional reasons we wouldn't be here," - here being a shop with a famous and expensive brand - "we'd be in The Goodwill Store, or The Shoe Discount Mega-Pavilion, or Wall*Mart, or Birkenstocks."

She breaths out of her mouth sharply in a derisive gesture that says, "What the hell do you know?" and continues trying on more pairs.

I get the feeling that my life is disappearing down a drain. Wasted. Minutes have become hours and we have nothing to show for it, no purchase, no entertainment and no education, unless one considers her implying that I'm an idiotic man has educational value for either of us.

"Look at them!" she says, turning her attention to a rack in the distance. I don't look at them, but she's not looking at me, she's looking at them. I've disappeared. She goes and gets "them". To me they're completely unexceptional. To her they're currently the Holy Grail, but I know that in two minutes they'll be just another heap of leather and packaging strewn across the floor.

I look around to see if anyone is watching us, seeing us vandalizing a store that was reasonably neat and organized when we entered it, but is now wilting under her unremitting attention. I feel my Saturday flowing away from me. A quarter of my weekend is already gone. My hard-earned weekend is seeping away like sand slipping through my fingers. Why did I come? Because we were going shopping for a pair of pants for me and, "well, nothing in particular," for her but she would "have a look around, maybe."

My pants were bought in two minutes max. The first pair she selected, the only pair I tried on were "great, perfect, really suit you, yes, wonderful," she said. I came shopping knowing what I wanted, I found it, I bought it. That's how men shop. Women go shopping on the basis that "I don't know what I want, but I'll know it when I see it (which is pretty similar to how a Supreme Court Justice defined pornography). As such, asking such questions as "What are you looking for?" is as useful as asking them to relate their purchase to the Special Theory of Relativity.

"Do you mind if we look in this shoe shop?" she asked, as we emerged from the store where I bought my pants, the first and only store that we went into that day that contained anything of interest to a heterosexual male.

"Of course not," I said, assuming I was returning the favor by accompanying her on a mundane shopping mission. I was duped, perhaps not intentionally, but I was duped nonetheless. During the course of the morning I came to hate the pants I'd bought, the bait. The bag containing them became glued to my hand over the next three hours, and I would look at it now and again, thinking "Traitors!"

We go to leave the latest shop, the fifteenth, the twentieth? As we walk past a huddle of shop assistants I sense that they're watching us, and I see one of them glance at the pile of mess we've left behind, and groan. As the expedition has worn on, my attempts to correct the damage before we leave a store have become less conscientious, and her own attempts to tidy up have been cursory at best.

In the first couple of shops I would ram shoes back into boxes as she discarded them, stuffing paper in randomly, but more or less putting the right shoes in the right boxes and returning them to a close approximation of where they should be on the shelves.

By the third shop I was less careful, and as her pace increased in shops four and five I could so barely keep up with her that I was ramming discarded shoes and paper into whatever box I could lay my hands on, then throwing them onto the shelves in any space available.

In shop six the two of us must have resembled a factory production line, with shoes being selected, unpacked, tried on, discarded, repacked and re-shelved at an astounding rate.

In shop eight I fell so far behind her that I gave up, and have kept my hands dug deeply and moodily in my pockets ever since, wandering along behind her and scuffing the ground with my shoes like a sulking adolescent.

I feel a tension between us, and when I feel it I know from experience that she's feeling it too, and also from experience I know that by the time I get to feel it, she's feeling angrier towards me than I am to her. She makes towards where the car is parked, away from the shops.

"Where are you going?" I ask. I don't need to ask, it's obvious from the silent, purposeful march away from the shops that she's saying, "I'm in a huff!" But I hope my fatuous question will start a discussion and avoid the path that we're currently heading down, the path to the inevitable silent, fuming resentment that will otherwise be fizzing between us for the rest of the day. I know I can calm things down and rescue the weekend if I say and do the right things for the next ten minutes. I'm just not sure that I want to.

"I could try one last shop, but you're obviously in some sort of a hurry," she says.

"Okay," I say. I don't add that not wanting to spend three hours looking for a pair of shoes doesn't necessarily equate to being in a hurry. Nor do I mention that for a person with over 50 pairs of shoes, one additional pair can hardly be seen as an urgent priority. Nor do I mention that ... but I stop myself as I start feeling my anger build again, and meekly follow her into the next shop.

My heart sinks. The place is enormous, and noisy with music. When did shops start taking background music out of the background and thrust it into the foreground? The old stuff was banal, but at least you could ignore it. Now they play music as part of the character of the store, so it's unignorable, it's loud, conversations must be shouted, and shouted conversations drown out the music, so the volume is cranked up, making the conversations become louder, and on and on, until you feel like going to a heavy metal concert for some peace and quiet. A piece of rap music starts up. I don't listen to the lyrics, but my ear catches an obscenity, then a stream of invective. "Did he say what I thought he said?" I ask, but nobody can hear me, I can't hear myself. Fortunately, the area we descend upon is quieter, so the ear damage will probably be moderate.

Before my girlfriend has the chance to grab a pair of shoes, an assistant is with us. This is going to be a problem. My girlfriend is a solo shopper. She goes about her selection process with extreme precision, and she doesn't need anyone to help her, not until it's practical matters such missing price tags or boxes too high to reach. She's a lone hit-woman, practiced in her art and dismissive of the support of others.

The assistant is a young girl. Attractive. Short skirt. Nice figure, a bit slimmer than girlfriend (worrying), bigger breasts (danger sign), and firmer butt (Red Alert!) – if the girl is any less sweet or more sexy than a 90-year-old nun there's going to be bad chemistry between them.

"Can I help you?" the girl says, then curiously in a louder voice adds "Or not?" She's staring at us in that manner that flight attendants have perfected over the years, the gaze that says "I'll do everything correctly on the surface, but behind this vacant look is a person you cannot fathom." This girl's visage says even more. Her scowl and her pout project arrogance and complete disinterest in her customers. The music collaborates with the scene, providing a thumping base that resembles thunder rumbling in the distance.

"No thank you," says my girlfriend. She doesn't look at the girl, and certainly doesn't add the perfunctory "we're just looking," which she considers to be a sign of weakness in the never-ending shopper-shopkeeper battle for psychological supremacy.

"What are you looking for?" the girl persists. Her tone of voice is a pretty good match for the flat drone that I used earlier to show how bored I was, and her body language – she's leaning against a rack inspecting her nails – is consummate in its expression of contrived unconcern.

At this point I should take her aside and give her some advice, some on-the-job training as it were, but I decide to stand back, knowing that the more pissed my girlfriend becomes with the assistant, the less anger she'll harbor towards me.

My girlfriend starts pulling out boxes. She looks around, I follow suit. There doesn't appear to be anywhere to sit whilst trying on the shoes.

"Where …?"

"The fitting area is at the back of the store," says the girl.

"The what?" says my girlfriend.

"The fitting area. You can try on the shoes there. It's equipped with mirrors at various angles so that you can see the shoes from all perspectives." She sounds as if she's reading a script. "And there are consultants who can discuss styles with you." She's gone from inspecting her nails to inspecting the face of her cell phone.

"Bloody hell," says my girlfriend. She hands me a couple of boxes and grabs a couple more for herself. "Come on," she says to me, "let's find this fabulous fitting area!"

"We have a policy," says the girl, scrolling through messages on her phone.

"Yes, I'm sure you do, everyone does, I have a policy that I only deal with polite shop assistants," says my girlfriend.

The girl seems to be focused on text messages on her phone, not on us. "Oh, I get it," she says to herself eventually, then she looks at us and says, "You are asked to take only three pairs at a time to the fitting area."

"Why?"

"To limit clutter."

"Then I'll try them on here," says my girlfriend, and plunks herself down on the floor, emphatically, but not very graciously. She starts trying on shoes. I'd like to intervene, to tell her that this really is a bit silly. But I keep quiet. There's a war brewing here, and I have the option of playing the role of cool and charming Switzerland.

The girl seems to be taking this in her stride and continues to show more interest in her nails, phone, hair and a few small flecks of white fluff on her tight black blouse than in the scene that's playing out on the floor at her feet. But despite her nonchalance, she continues her narration of the shop policy, and there's a slight hardening of tone as the litany proceeds.

"We discourage customers from trying on shoes in the aisles, as it creates congestion and hinders the access of other customers to the displays," she intones.

"Look around," says my girlfriend, turning her head from side to side whilst pulling off one shoe and pulling on another. "Do you see anyone being obstructed?"

She's wearing a skirt, and as she contorts herself on the floor I catch glimpses of the top of her thigh, which is fine by me because she's got fine thighs, but I can't say that it conveys a great sense of decorum.

"If you don't take your three pairs of shoes to the fitting area, I'll have to call the manager."

"Then call the damn manager so that he, she or it can explain your weird policies to me!"

"Most people behave reasonably," the girl says.

I wince. That isn't the language I would have chosen under the circumstances. I would bet money on the fact that an eruption is imminent. I picture the two of them rolling around the floor of the store in a desperate bundle of scratching and clawing, of punching and slapping, of kicking and head butting. I'm embarrassed, but comfortable in the fact that my role is now purely peripheral. Compared to the rancor between the two of them, the irritability that existed between my girlfriend and I ten minutes ago has the relative magnitude of a minor squabble between infants at the height of a global nuclear war.

But, as always, women never cease to surprise me.

"Those look good on you," says the girl.

All three of us look at my girlfriend's feet.

"They do," I say, not altogether lying.

"And they're comfortable," says my girlfriend.

"And they're on sale, 25% off, today only," says the girl.

There's a long pause, whilst all three of us stare at her feet again.

"Okay," says my girlfriend. "I'll take them." I feel as if the Cuban Missile Crisis has been defused. We can all sleep safe in our beds again.

We pay. We go.

"That bitch," says my girlfriend as we're driving home.

"Yes," I say. Not agreeing with her, but just relieved.

"But they're beautiful shoes."

"Yes," I say, feeling as if I've got off lightly.

When we get home I angrily throw my trousers into a closet. It's at least a month before I feel like wearing them, and when I do the zipper breaks – I'll have to take them back to the shop. •

Seeing red

Red for heat, red for stop, red for blood. Like a red rag to a bull.

Well, bulls don't see in color, so any old color of cloth flicked at its face and around its head will get it mad.

When you get really angry and emotional, the blood rises to the surface, and you see through a red mist - hence seeing red.

Liar

The guy I was talking to was looking over my shoulder at something taking place behind me, and I was looking over his shoulder at something taking place behind him. Obviously this was not a conversation that was going anywhere. We mumbled some pleasant parting remarks, "Good to talk to you" or "Enjoy the party" or some such inanity, whereas we could really have said, "I hope you crash your car on the way home and die a painful death" or "Your wife is upstairs screwing a guy she met five minutes ago." It was all just party-speak. As I wandered through the mêlée I picked up scraps of conversation, little aphorisms designed for sound-bite conversations, built to impress, even when uttered over Miles Davis and from a mouth working on chicken meat and Chardonnay.

"I was invited to the inauguration, but I had more important things to do."

"And I told him where to stick his job. I don't need that sort of thing any more."

"Ethics are very important to me. I would always take an ethical job over an unethical one, assuming the pay was okay."

"She was like something out of Baywatch, and all over me, really, it was amazing. I just couldn't cool her down ..."

I went to get a fresh drink and found Lucy in the kitchen. We wandered around the party deciding which little group to join. We'd been dating for three months or so. It had been hot and heavy from the outset, and I thought I knew her pretty well, but maybe I was confusing physical intimacy with mental intimacy, passion outvoting logic.

It wasn't a very loud party. You could talk to people and hear what they said back.

We joined a group with two other couples. They were strangers, and I can't say I liked the look of them very much. The men were loud and flashy. The women looked as though they had stepped out of Vogue and were dripping with Gucci and Swarovski. The two women occasionally whispered to each other and laughed conspiratorially. The two men occasionally whispered to each other and laughed lewdly.

One of the couples evidently had a 14-year-old son who had recently taken his mother's car out for a joyride.

"He thought we were gone for the day," the mother of the delinquent was saying. "But I was home early, out in the front yard pruning the roses, and I saw him drive up, large as life, looking as if he'd been driving for years, swigging out of a can of coke as he screeched into the drive at about 40 miles an hour!

"He didn't see me at first, then one of his pals – he had a goddam car full of buddies with him, two of them drinking beer – one of his pals spotted me, and all the doors flew open and his buddies are off and running. He thought about running himself, so I yelled 'Justin! Get the hell over here! And he stops in his tracks and turns round and says, 'Oh, hi Mom, how's it going?' And I said, 'How's it fucking going?' Yeah, I shouldn't have swore, but I was about to tear the little S.O.B. into shreds."

"Hold it Mary," said one of the men, "did I just hear you refer to your offspring as an S.O.B.?"

They all laughed, and laughed far more than the observation deserved, showing the dedication half-drunk partygoers give to having a good time no matter what.

"Anyhow," the woman continued, "I'm ranting and raving at the kid, telling him I'm going to cut off his privileges, walking round the car looking at the holy mess inside, dragging him along with me. Then he struggles free and backs off and says, 'Mom, don't do anything hasty now,' and I yell at him some more, then I notice he's looking real scared, staring at me, at my hand in particular, and I say, 'What's the matter?' and he says, 'What you mean when you say you're gonna cut off my privileges?', and I look at what he's staring at, and it's the rose pruners that I've got gripped in my hand that I've been waving about as I've been yelling at him. The kid thinks I'm gonna cut off … well, I can only guess what he thought I was gonna cut off!"

More laughter, and I joined in, just to be sociable really. As details were being added and the laughter prolonged, Lucy interjected. "I'm sorry, but I don't find this amusing. My cousin was killed in a crash with an underage driver."

Silence. I looked at her face, which was quite expressionless, but I thought I detected the hint of a wry smile. A sad smile, I supposed. My knowledge of her told me that she was basically a fun-loving person, the last one to pour cold water on an occasion, so I inferred that she had been deeply affected by her cousin's death. The whole roomful of people seemed to fall quiet, not just the group we were in.

The two women excused themselves to go to the bathroom, and the two men excused themselves to top up their drinks, which were already topped up enough. Within 20 seconds of her making the remark about her cousin, Lucy and I were standing alone in the middle of the room, aware that just about everyone there was watching us but trying not to show it. A wave of embarrassment flowed around the house so we left about a half-hour later. Our car was parked a way down the road where there were no streetlights. As I opened it up Lucy grabbed me in an embrace that left me in no doubt as to what she wanted, and wanted urgently. We got into the back of the car and she had my pants undone before I could blink. Then she was on top of me, making love frantically, almost violently.

On the drive home I said, "Sorry about your cousin."

"What cousin?" she replied absently, still combing her hair after our tussle.

"I didn't know you had a cousin who was killed in a car crash."

"I don't," she said. "I mean I didn't," she added, correcting her grammar.

"But you ... I ... You don't?"

"Didn't," she said, now correcting me and laughing.

"But you said ... you said you did," I stammered.

"Yes," she said, her tone of voice telling me that she was uninterested in the subject.

"Why?"

"Oh, those people were odious, pompous," she said. "Can we get high when we get back to your place? I feel like partying."

• • •

Lying bothers me a lot. Why would anyone lie to another person? Sure, there are crooks, who need to do it, but I'm not a crook, and I don't want to associate with anyone who is. Sometimes white lies are excusable, like telling someone that they look great when they look just okay but have put a lot of effort into looking that way. Apart from that, it's insulting to be lied to, as if you don't deserve the respect of being told the truth.

The incident at the party (together with the way she so casually and erotically shrugged it off afterwards) stayed in my mind, and for a few days it troubled me a lot, to the extent that I started to question our relationship in a way I never had before. I resolved to raise it with her. But somehow the discussion never happened. I chickened out, I guess. That and the fact that the rest of our relationship was so thoroughly satisfying. We liked to do the same things at the same times. We chatted easily and creatively about interesting issues, not just about trivia. She helped me start looking for another job. She was insightful and supportive, giving me a confidence that I didn't previously have, raising my expectations as to what I could do. She helped me build an image of myself that made me feel more capable. Thus did I come to rely upon her, and I didn't really question the fact that she was making me appear to be something I wasn't. If her clever rewriting of my CV didn't get me a great job, nothing would.

Basically we just liked to be with each other, and the sex was simply superb.

Anyway, for whatever reason, cowardice or hedonism or happenstance, the incident at the party faded into the background and the fundamental concern that "She tells lies" I managed to tone down into "She tells other people lies", and then added "as a matter of convenience," but that clause didn't really add anything – a lie is a lie is a lie.

• • •

Summer arrived, and her parents were due to visit her. They wanted to meet me and I really wanted to meet them. I realized that I wanted to meet them, not just for obvious reasons, but also because they would give me some additional reference points on her. I didn't relate this directly to the incident at the party, but more to the fact that I didn't know any of her friends very well, and had met none of her relatives, and for whatever reason we had never discussed our backgrounds very much. We lived in the present, and that was another intoxicating part of our relationship, particularly for me, a person who is too easily distracted by the disappointments of the past and the challenges of the future.

"You'll like my father," she said. "He's a down-to-earth guy. He's a mail man."

"He's a what?" I said.

"A mail carrier, works for the USPS."

"But you told me he was a surgeon!" I felt myself go cold. The glint in her eye, which usually so beguiled me, at once became mischievous, ominous.

"So?" she said, teasingly.

I fumbled to find words. I didn't want this conversation to be happening.

"I thought ... but ... did he used to be a surgeon before he was a mail man?" I asked, flailing to find another explanation and not have to confront the one that was staring me in the face.

"No!" she said, laughing heartily, and even slapping her thigh in her mirth.

"But why did you ... why did you tell me he was?"

"I was flirting," she said. "I wanted you."

"But you lied!"

"What damage has it done? We hooked up. We're having a great time."

I said nothing. I couldn't speak.

"Look," she said, "when we started dating you wore smart clothes. Now look at you!"

I was wearing shorts and a t-shirt, both of which had seen better days. The t-shirt even had a sizeable stain on it.

"You put on a pretence back then," she said, "and so did I. I used language, you used Eddie Bauer and Banana Republic!"

Again, I looked down at my threadbare denim shorts, which had gone from being an irrelevance to a major point of contention in just a few seconds.

Her argument was fatuous. To compare barefaced lies with societal conventions was absurd, a reversal of reality, like calling Winston Churchill a war criminal and Adolph Hitler a freedom fighter. But she was calm, in control, and I wasn't. I sensed that I might be able to win the argument if I could pull myself together, but I would ruin the relationship, and she looked so damn good that night!

• • •

I got over it to the extent that our relationship kept going, although I was like a man who had eaten a gourmet meal but who now felt as if he was about to suffer indigestion – I'd had a good experience and didn't want to spoil it, but there was something uncomfortable in the background that, try as I might, I couldn't ignore. When I was with her, enjoying her company and the version of me that she provoked, enjoying her body and the things that we did together, I was okay. But when I thought about her at any other time it was as though a hard lump formed in my stomach, a knot of anxiety and a tangible reminder that she had lied, and had lied to me personally.

I met her parents. They were in their early 60s. Her mother was quiet, refined, smiling, assured – I liked her. Her father was a chatterbox. He just loved to talk, sometimes engagingly, sometimes not. He was a bit of a bigot, a bit of a racist, a bit homophobic, but knew he shouldn't be any of these things and was always correcting himself when he strayed onto dangerous turf. Actually, it was amusing to see him start expressing extreme views and then watch him drag himself back on course as if he was slapping his errant opinions into a more liberal shape.

At one convivial dinner he conducted the following monologue, all of the promptings and course corrections coming from himself, with just the occasional bland but meaningful glance from his wife.

"I sure wouldn't like to be seen to by a queer male nurse. I mean, not queer, I mean, can you say "queer" now? Is that okay. These frigging words are okay one day and bad the next then okay again.

Know what I mean? Anyhow, homo then, no, I mean gay. Yeah, gay. I wouldn't like that. I mean for a proctology or prostate stuff. I mean, for a broken leg ... no, not leg, let's say finger. For a finger it would be fine. But then, hell, I mean, there'd be other people around, wouldn't there? I mean, even if the nurse was a raving faggot, no, I mean even if he was a real gay, gay guy, then he'd have to behave, wouldn't he? Like when you're seen to by a female nurse, she couldn't do nothing weird neither, could she? Not that I'd mind in that case. I mean, not if she was good looking. Ha! Or even if she weren't good looking, I wouldn't see her face if she was fiddling about down there, would I? Ha ha. No, no, really. I'd be fine with a gay nurse, you know, in company. Yeah. Sure I would."

Lucy rolled her eyes. Her mother shook her head. I laughed.

It diluted the pleasure of the visit that I was continually looking for hints as to Lucy's character. I applied extreme attention to any stories about her past, and I had to forcefully restrain myself from probing too deeply when I saw any area that might expose more details regarding her integrity.

On the penultimate evening of their stay, Lucy wanted to spend some time with her mother, shopping, eating chocolate cake and so forth, leaving her father and me to go drinking, and drink we did.

He was an amiable drunk. Freed of the constraints of political correctness his language became more amusing and somewhat more outrageous, but without ever becoming more than slightly insulting to any particular gender, sexual orientation, race, class or creed, and healthy self-deprecation was a recurring theme.

We laughed a lot, and he cried a little as he told me about the child of theirs that had died when only 3-days-old.

"I can see her little hands clutching at the air to this day, as if she was trying to hold on to life that was slipping away from her."

We covered a lot of ground that evening, but most of it related to our opinions regarding things of no consequence personally, like sports, cars, movies, politics and so forth, and with only the occasional oblique reference to the budding relationship between his daughter and me, things like, "You'll have to come and visit us in Ohio sometime."

But I realized that he was subtly opening me up, learning my opinions on a range of subjects and my reactions to his. I don't know if this was intentional, but if it was it was deftly handled.

We were on our last drink, one for the road. I don't recall how we got onto the subject of Lucy's career, but at one point he said:

"Lucy's going to be promoted to Director, I hear, from Office Manager. Not bad, eh? I guess that's where the brains in the family ended up," and he went on to talk about his dropout son, but I was no longer listening.

Lucy wasn't an office manager. She was a sales assistant in a gift shop, one of those shops where you can never work out how they stay in business – all they sold were staggeringly mundane greetings cards and useless, overpriced trinkets.

Luckily I was drunk and my mind was slowed down to a crawl, so that although I'd clearly absorbed what he'd said, I didn't react, I just brooded inwardly as he rambled on about the son who couldn't seem to hold down a job for more than two weeks.

I went home, drank a couple of pints of water and took two heavy-duty sleeping pills, hoping to calm and divert my racing brain from the mantra that it was repeating over and over again: "She lies to others. She lies to her family. She lies to me. She's a compulsive liar."

● ● ●

I didn't see her the next day, but she was on my mind for all of it. Not just on my mind, but at the center of my every thought. The following day, Saturday, we'd planned to go looking at apartments. We were thinking of moving in together, and neither of our existing apartments was big enough to accommodate both of us. I got to her place around 11 a.m. I had no intention of going apartment hunting. She poured me a cup of coffee.

"Why do you tell your father you're an office manager?"

"Ha! He said that, did he? He just says that to make me look better, and to make him look better."

"He lies?"

"So what? It's harmless."

"You lie," I reminded her. Her eyes flashed.

"Ditto. Trivial stuff. Like father, like daughter," she said, dismissively.

It crossed my mind that she was lying again now, that her father wasn't lying and that she'd actually told him that she was an office manager, which would mean that she was not only lying to me again, but also making her own father look like a liar. The alternative was that she was telling the truth and her father was also a liar, which meant that I was getting tangled up, not with just one liar, but with a whole family of them! My head was spinning.

"I can't handle this. I can't handle your lying. You. Your father. It's just too much."

"Take a look at your résumé," she said. Her voice was calm, but her eyes were boring into me.

"What?"

"You updated it when you were applying for that job a few weeks ago. It's bullshit. It's a grain of serious truth with a big fat smile plastered over it, and the smile is a lie. When we're talking about the business world you tell me that it's crap, a fraud, greedy, nasty, that you can't wait to make a pile then get out and leave all the shit behind. Then in your résumé you say you're dedicated to your work, enthusiastic, ambitious to succeed, committed and thoroughly loyal to any company you work for." The words stung me as she recited them, almost verbatim, from my résumé.

"You lie," she continued. "Lying doesn't stop being lying just because a load of people do it. You just think that your sort of lying is okay but mine isn't. That makes you a liar and a hypocrite!"

She was right, but she was also wrong, and I thought she was more wrong than right, but I was too confused to weigh things up sensibly.

"But why do you have to do it?"

"Did your parents tell you about Santa Claus?" she asked.

I didn't answer. Of course they did.

"That was a lie," she continued, assuming the obvious. "But it made your life richer. It made you happy and it made them happy. Fairy stories are lies, the theater and movies are lies, fiction is a lie, Shakespeare was a consummate liar, re-writing history to suit his career progression."

"That's different," I said, not really knowing what I meant by that.

"You like to be in control, don't you?" she asked. "You like things to be black and white. Well, wake up! The world isn't like that. It's full of shades of gray, and if you really want to be black and white, why is it okay to tell the conventional lies but not the others? You tell your boss he's right when you know he's wrong, and you defend that by saying it's just being diplomatic, part of building a career. Okay, so it may be, but it's also a lie."

Silence. My mind was buzzing. I was outraged, incensed, but also vulnerable, adrift, and desperately in need of an anchor. I felt like Alice after she stepped through the looking glass. Down is up and up is down. Values aren't solid things, they are views, choices, and they can be changed on a whim. No, I couldn't believe that, but something was pulling me in that direction, and it had nothing to do with right and wrong, somehow it felt much more momentous than one man's interpretation of correctness.

She took my hand in both of hers, looked me straight in the eye, and said:

"I love you, and that's no lie," and I instinctively knew that it wasn't.

"I love you too," I said.

"Are you sure?"

"Yes," I said, hoping I was telling the truth.

We went out to look at apartments and found one that she loved and I quite liked, but I said I loved it, just to be supportive.

Throughout my life I'd always deeply loved my father, but at regular intervals, particularly during adolescence, I had really and honestly wanted to kill him. Honesty comes at a price, but I guess love just costs a lot more. •

Blaise Pascal: Imagination

"Imagination disposes of everything; it creates beauty, justice and happiness, which are everything in this world."

Blaise Pascal was French. He was a child prodigy, born in 1623, and lived a mere 2 months beyond his 39th birthday.

Pascal initially devoted his intelligence to maths and science, his work influencing today's economics and social science.

Throughout his life he suffered ill-health, which led him to focus on religion. After a near-death experience he turned to philosophy. He wrote the controversial Provincial Letters, which attacked the kind of reasoning Catholic thinkers would use to justify their behavior. For example, they would argue that lying is fine if it saves a life, even though they would agree that lying is morally wrong.

Winds of change

Flatulence. A natural bodily function, but a social taboo. A huge relief, but a huge embarrassment. A subject that's eschewed by the majority, but delighted in by a fanatical minority (which includes all males between the ages of zero and 20, and all rugby players up to the time of death – in fact, the goal of every rugby player is to die mid-fart with a pint of Guinness by their side).

But the aim of this piece is not to engage in lavatory humor. If it were, you would be reading it in some other book, not in this masterpiece collection (at least I claimed its superior excellence in the letter proposing the book to the publisher). No, the aim of this piece is to review the importance of flatulence in respect of relationships.

Think of a relationship you have had or are having, one that's lasted for more than 12 hours. If you've had more than one, you have a choice to make. If you've never had one, then just imagine, or ask a friend, or go and commit suicide, which is probably what you think of doing most days anyway.

In the overwhelming majority of cases, you did not establish the relationship on the basis of wind emission (presence, absence, timeliness, reaction to, volume of, bouquet, etc.). In fact, I can go further than this and say that the subject didn't come up at all on the first date, and probably took some time to emerge.

Actually, there are several cases on record of couples who have been living together for years and who have never mentioned the subject overtly. It's been thought about, reacted to, agonized over to be sure, but mentioned, never. Needless to say, these case records are to be found in psychiatrists' offices, because any relationship of significant duration that has not confronted the issue of digestive gas ejection is obviously completely screwed up. (Note: I say "confronted", not "addressed", let alone "settled". Resolving the issue is an aspiration that few achieve, and not without substantial intake of prescription medicines and/or artificial stimulants).

Anyway, in most relationships, the subject comes up at some point, and scientists have determined that the bedroom is the most likely location for matters to come to a head (or a nose). The bedroom is the place where fart-awareness most commonly reaches the "olfactory crisis point", which is defined as being the stage at which ignoring the event is more perverse than recognizing it, unless you are either Ms. Manners or the Queen of England.

This isn't surprising. Ninety-nine percent of the things that scientists claim to "discover" are things which the rest of us pretty much took for granted anyway. How often do you read of something completely extraordinary that scientists have discovered; such as that water runs uphill in a remote region of Mongolia, or that there is a woman in a small tribe in Borneo who, whilst suffering from PMS, embedded an axe in her partner's head, and then actually regretted it?

But I digress. Let's get back to bedroom flatulence and dispel a few myths:

1) What smells okay to you may not smell okay to anyone else, particularly not someone who is just finding out that you are not perfect after all, at least not in the area of digestive processes. (Note: as you've found your way to the bedroom, you've most probably had sex, therefore, there is almost certainly one other area where your imperfections have already been displayed, so don't blame your poor old stomach for being the first one to let the cat out of the bag).

2) Fanning of sheets does help to disperse the odor more rapidly. However, stomach gases don't seem to follow the established rules of physics in this regard, in that the odor doesn't become weaker by dilution, but it actually becomes stronger (and, of course, a bloody sight more noticeable). It's as if

stomach gas molecules manage to persuade or bully adjacent air molecules into getting on the bandwagon and joining in the fun, so that what began as an emission that occupied a few cubic liters is soon enough to fill a space the size of a football stadium, and expanding at the speed of an exploding dirty bomb.

3) There is nothing else on earth that sounds like air passing through a person's rear, so trying to create a pathetic diversionary sound by scratching a sheet, snoring, coughing, etc. simply makes you look sillier than you already look.

4) If you allow a dog into the bedroom, then you have a great alibi. You can easily blame a dog for silent flatulence, and the dog will actually take great pride in assuming ownership. I used to know a spaniel that would sniff its backside quizzically whenever any new smell was in evidence (good smells simply sent it running for the kitchen), and would look positively crestfallen if it didn't prove to be the source of the eye-watering stench. However, this strategy has a downside. Dogs do get flatulent and, given their diet of 50% meat, 40% trash and 10% postal carriers' body parts, when they let off you may wonder if a dose of personal embarrassment isn't preferable to inhaling a gas that can dissolve lung tissue.

5) Phrases such as "better out than in," references to Chaucer's and Ben Jonson's interests in farting, and other proverbial or classical allusions to the condition will not get you off the hook. Claims of suffering excruciating pain through the withholding of offensive vapors will not, of themselves, evoke sympathy, but are more likely to result in shouts of "go to the doctor!" delivered from a safe distance or even from another room, or (in extreme cases) via a mediating attorney.

Now let's move on to the serious matter of how flatulence can be accommodated in a long term relationship (i.e. greater than three months for most of us, or greater than three days for lotharios, misogynists or college students). A typical flowchart of behaviors is as follows (in chronological order):

1) Acknowledgement that the partner passes wind. (Note: if this acknowledgement is never made, you obviously have no sense of smell, so you have many other problems in life, but not this particular one)

2) One of the following then applies:

   a. EITHER acceptance that the partner can do it whenever they like, (Note: in this case, you're a veritable saint – you should stop reading this and go back to watching re-runs of Deepak Chopra on PBS, to which you are surely a paid-up subscriber).

   b. OR realization that the issue (no pun intended) must be discussed – go to (3) below.

   c. OR realization that it is impossible to have a relationship with a person having stomach content of which that stench is representative – go to (4) below.

3) Discuss matter and:

   a. EITHER agree on acceptable limits (e.g. only in the bathroom, or two toxic releases allowed after Indian food or refried beans, or advanced warnings must be given, or restrictions lifted during earthquakes or when confronted with other life-threatening situations).

   b. OR have a huge row – go to (4) below.

   c. OR (the majority situation) agree that flatulence will always be a source of contention and one that will be argued over throughout the relationship, but is not, of itself, likely to lead to the end of the relationship (unless inebriated partner raises discussion of your gastro-effusive performance at dinner parties or other social gatherings).

4) End relationship, go and join an ashram that exists on a vegan diet (heavy on the legumes), realize that your partner was an amateur compared to your new-found guru, go back and try for a reconciliation, write to an advice column, take Prozac.

So there it is, relationships, flatulence and everything in between (with a few minor exceptions) presented and discussed in a nutshell, with scientific validation throughout. If what you've read here isn't enough to protect the love of your life from the vicissitudes of your digestive tract, take my advice and buy a dog, the bigger the better. •

Offensive or not?

On stepping into the elevator, the businessman quickly detected an offensive odor. The only other occupant was a little old lady.

"Excuse me," he addressed her, "did you happen to pass wind?"

"Of course I did," she replied. "You don't think I stink like this all the time do you?"

Painting the deck

"Let's paint the deck," she said, enthusiastically.

"Why?" I asked, cautiously.

"What is it made from?" she asked, avoiding my question and parrying it with one of her own.

"Redwood," I said, sticking to the facts. "Californian Redwood."

"What color is it?" she asked, sticking to some other agenda.

I looked at the deck. We were sitting on it, having a glass or two of wine. I spent hours of every day gazing vacantly at the deck and the view that it was part of, but this time I paid it special attention.

"Gray," I answered, still sticking to the facts.

"Exactly!" she cried, triumphantly. "But it should be red," as if I needed to have it explained to me.

"Things go gray as they age. As they age gracefully. Like hair. Are you saying I should start treating my hair with henna," I said, smugly.

She looked at my head. Her look said "might not be a bad idea" but she said nothing. She didn't need to.

"One or the other of us spills a glass of wine on it every now and again. We just have to stick to red wine and make it a bit more methodical."

"Brilliant," she said, sarcastically.

"Have you ever seen the inside of a red wine barrel?" I parried. "Deep red, luscious smell. Now that would be some deck!"

"Be serious."

"It's a big job," I said, immediately regretting it. I had stupidly given ground and allowed us to go from "why paint the deck" to "how do we paint the deck" without putting up enough of a struggle. I cursed myself. Then I cursed her, silently, of course.

We looked through catalogs. We looked at tones of stain. We selected the cleaning appliance (to rent). We even decided upon when we would do it. More thought went into painting the bloody deck than into any other single component of our relationship.

"What should I wear?" she asked one morning over breakfast.

"For what?" I asked, expecting it to be on account of some party, or dinner, or other significant occasion.

"For when we paint the deck," she answered, with that "isn't it bloody obvious" expression that I've come to know so well.

"Well, you don't want to get any of your good clothes messed up," I said, "so why don't you wear some of mine?" It was intended as a joke.

"Good idea," she said, not a flicker of amusement on her face.

Day one arrives, the cleaning day. Day 2 will be a rest day (and probably either a relationship rebuilding day or one of moody silence). Day 3 will be the painting day, and days four to ten will be further relationship rebuilding days, I estimate, based on past experience. With luck, in two weeks we should have a newly painted deck and a relationship that's back where it started before she first said, "Let's paint the deck."

We swept, and in so doing we realized that there was a load of debris stuck between the planks, debris that we should really get rid of before we started washing. So we spent the next two hours on our hands and knees on what was fast becoming a baking hot deck, running saw blades between the planks to clean out the crap that had accumulated between them. There are a lot of long planks on my deck and, therefore, a lot of long spaces between them. In total, we probably crawled along several miles of crack. It was slow, hot work, and a job we hadn't reckoned on. It was past 11 a.m. We'd already sweat-soaked our way through one set of clothes, we still had to go and collect the pressure washer, and pressure of another sort was already building between us.

"You missed that bit," she said, pointing past me.

"You missed that bit," I responded, pointing past her.

"What about over there?" she said, pointing elsewhere.

"Or over there?" I replied, pointing at random to a part of her territory.

"We have different standards," she said, and it was then I realized that much of the criticism we would be leveling at each other over our deck resurfacing skills, was really aimed much more personally. The deck repainting was to be a surrogate upon which to perform a detailed analysis of our relationship. Nations fight out battles in the sports arena as they might once have fought on the battleground. We were about to embark on a similar challenge, although I worried it would end up more like a war than a sporting event.

We decided to call it quits regarding the crud between the planks. We agreed that it was "good enough" and we needed to get on with the washing.

LESSON ONE: Relationships must be able to accommodate differences of opinion and differences of standards, and must be able to accept compromises (even when you know you're damn well right and your partner is just being bloody awkward.)

We set off for Home Depot to rent the pressure washer. What I thought was going to be a simple exercise turned into a lesson in hydraulics, physics, turbulent liquid flow theory, mechanical engineering, and plumbing. After the man in the rental department had given us a long demonstration of how to work the washer, we looked at each other, looked at him, and said, "Can you show us that again?" He did so, without flinching visibly.

"So you suck the detergent up with this thing?" asked Eleanor, holding the end of a pipe.

"No," I said, confidently, maybe even a bit dismissively, "that's the sprayer."

"No," said the man, "that's the water feed."

"Oh," I said, abashed, glancing at Eleanor to see if I could spot a complacent grin – I couldn't, but I'm sure one was lurking there somewhere.

"Can you show us again?" we asked.

We received a total of four complete or partial demonstrations before the man said he had to take his lunch break. I didn't believe him, but I didn't blame him either – it probably wasn't every day that he encountered two such accomplished mechanical morons.

"I have 50% confidence that we know how to work the damn thing," I said in the car on the way home.

"I have 100%," she declared, somewhat haughtily. I automatically (but silently) divided her 100% number by four, based on her past demonstrations of confidence versus capability in mechanical matters.

LESSON TWO: Equilibrium can be maintained if one retains a modest and balanced demeanor at all times (and keeps one's mouth firmly shut despite provocative claims).

The deck-washing went reasonably well, with a couple of exceptions. Firstly, only one of us could use the machine at a time, whereas both of us had set aside the entire day for the exercise. We were both dressed for it, focused on it, and not expecting to do anything else, so we tended to fall into the configuration of one spraying and the other watching, and, as the devil makes work for idle hands (and mouths), the watcher soon became the critic. The way the spraying person overcame this irritation (and although I speak for myself here, I would bet jackpot lottery winnings on the fact that she had the same strategy) was to inadvertently direct the reflected spray from the washer in the direction of the watching person. One was able to do this with the ostensible excuse of diligently attending to the deficiency that the watcher had just pointed out, so they could hardly complain if the resulting spray-cloud rinsed them, could they?

Secondly, despite ordering more than enough detergent to cover the whole of the deck twice over, I miscalculated the rate of application and ran out of detergent half-way through. Needless to say, my attention was drawn to this fact immediately, and then at regular intervals for the next two weeks. Even now, months after the last drop of sealant was applied and the brushes cleaned, whenever someone visits and remarks on our nice deck, they are told that, "Yes, it is nice, isn't it. Pity we ran out of detergent and didn't wash it completely." As long as she continues to use the "we" in this statement I'll be able to grin and bear it, but if a "he" ever creeps in, I'm not sure that I'll be so sanguine.

LESSON THREE: Take and offer criticism constructively (within the earshot of your partner, that is).

We got to the end of the cleaning phase. Actually, it didn't go too badly. I managed to withhold most criticism of Eleanor's ability to aim the cleaning wand, beyond pointing out that I thought it was a good idea of hers to "clean a 100 yard radius beyond the deck at the same time, including the cat." She, likewise, was restrained, apart from telling me that it was a good idea of mine to "get crap all over the windows to the house, because it will keep the sun out and make for a cooler environment within, thereby saving on energy bills, which is obviously your main goal in life, bar none."

At the end of the day the deck looked good. We were tired but happy, in the way that two people who have worked hard together towards a common goal can be. Differences were forgotten (albeit temporarily), and satisfaction at the joint effort predominated. Even the man at Home Depot seemed to share some of our pleasure, although in his case it was probably more due to the fact that he hadn't received a continuous stream of panicky phone calls from us throughout the day, and his machine had been returned in a mostly serviceable condition.

We were content, and the next day was a peaceful hiatus. Then came Day Three, Saturday, the painting day.

We emerged onto the deck at around 10 a.m. with two huge cans of some expensive, Brazilian, oil-based sealant that someone had persuaded us to buy. The day was already hot and the deck was completely unshaded. The first thing that I read in the instructions printed large on the side of the can was, "Do not apply in hot, sunny conditions."

There was no explanation as to why one should follow this clear instruction. Would the sealant not take? Would it decompose, damaging the wood and emitting potentially poisonous vapors in the process? Would it dry on contact and fail to penetrate? This was serious. No point "spoiling the ship for a ha'peth of tar". Given the work we'd put into the cleaning, and work we were about to put into the painting, and the investment we'd put into both, we should do it properly. It was a damn nuisance, but we had to do this properly. I told Eleanor, conveying the need for us to consider this carefully.

"Screw that," she said, and started painting. I stood dumbstruck for fully two minutes, then did the same, quietly admiring her straightforward approach, but anxious that it might be just a little too straightforward in this context.

LESSON FOUR: Pragmatism is essential in maintaining the smooth flow of a relationship (sometimes you just have to do as you're told).

I was equipped with a tray and a roller to cover the horizontal surfaces. Eleanor was armed with brushes to paint the railings and the more fiddly nooks and crannies. For quite some time I was worried that we'd arrived at this allocation of tasks by way of gender stereotypes. I didn't used to think much about gender stereotypes, but Eleanor is very big on this subject, and although I can't say that

she's communicated some of her enthusiasm for the subject to me, she has force-fed me with enough of the bloody stuff that I give it more than the occasional thought, and certainly more thought than I would like to give it.

Why was I using the large implement to cover the big, visible surfaces, whilst she was using the small tools on the more subtle, detailed areas? Big and bold versus small and dainty. We hadn't really discussed it, we just seemed naturally to assume these roles. As I considered this at length, I looked across to see Eleanor happily slapping sealant on the woodwork, discordantly singing "It's not unusual" à la Tom Jones, apparently without a care in the world. This caused me to worry about role reversal in the other direction – she being the devil-may-care one and me being the worrier-over-detail.

Then either the attention to the job in hand quieted my mind, or maybe the heat distracted me, or perhaps the fumes from the pungent sealant were pleasantly anesthetizing my overactive brain, because the next thing I was aware of was her calling out, "Let's have a break" about an hour later.

LESSON FIVE: Don't second-guess. Take things as they appear to be. Worrying over "what-ifs" can create tensions where none previously existed and for no valid reason (i.e. don't be paranoid!).

I looked at her, then at myself. She was doing the same. I had a few splashes of the red-brown sealant on my shoes and pants. She looked as though she'd been a bad loser in a paint-ball fight, a full 25% of her body area covered with sealant splatter.

"Did you have to pick that t-shirt?" I asked, trying not to sound annoyed. There must be 20 t-shirts in my closet, some of them in an advanced state of decay and perfect candidates for dirty jobs. On a top shelf, well away from the used t-shirts, there are five or six t-shirts, still in their original wrappings. Unused. Pristine. It was one

of these she had chosen to use.

"Why not?" she replied. "You said to use your clothes." I can't be certain, but I think I detected a smirk hovering in the background.

An exotic, Brazilian, oil-based sealant, designed by God to protect trees from the ravages of the equatorial rain forest, and designed by Home Depot to keep the fury of the elements out of my deck for the next five years, is hardly likely to succumb to a pathetic household washing detergent. Which means that the filthy state of my brand new t-shirt was likely to be the one that it would be in for the remainder of its life.

"Did you have to stand on a chair to get that down?" I asked. Knowing I should swallow hard and drop the subject.

"What?" she replied; that single word conveying both "what are you talking about?" and "I can't believe we're having this conversation!" and probably lots more besides.

"There are loads of old t-shirts within reach when you open my closet, yet you chose to pick a new one from an inaccessible height, a height for which you probably had to get a chair to be able to reach, which demonstrates that a good deal of thought went into picking one of my new t-shirts to do a shitty job when a more appropriate solution was, quite literally, staring you in the face." I shouldn't have said that, but having said it I should definitely have stopped there. I didn't.

"This being the case," I continued, "how do you think I should interpret your decision to make a choice that seems on the face of it to be perverse, malicious, vindictive, or just plain stupid."

There was a pause.

"I'll get the coffee," she said, and walked off to the kitchen. "Would you like a cookie with it?" she called back to me, pleasantly, smiling.

LESSON SIX: Refusing to engage in an argument can appear annoying to your partner, but it is sometimes the best way of defusing what could otherwise turn into a serious confrontation. (i.e. reckon on knuckle-clenching frustration as being an integral part of any lasting relationship).

Halfway through the afternoon and three quarters way across the deck, it started to look as if we might run out of sealant. An hour later it was a sure thing. There was no doubt who could get cleaned up first and go and buy another can – the surface area of Eleanor was by then more sealant than not.

"I suppose we could always wring out your t-shirt," I told her. "That would give us another pint or two."

"Speaking of which," she said, "could I have another shirt? This one is yucky."

"No," I said, and set off for the shop feeling reasonably confident that when I got back she would be wearing a fresh shirt, another of my new ones.

LESSON SEVEN: Don't prejudge (i.e. it's bad enough when it actually happens – there's no need to brood on it in advance, and there's a slight possibility that the worst won't happen, but don't bank on it).

I got the paint, she picked one of my t-shirts, but it was an old one, and I dare say we'll be able to clean the sealant handprints off the closet doors in due course. We finished the deck. It looked really good. I was glad she'd suggested that we paint it. We had a drink to celebrate, then another, feeling tired but as if we'd accomplished something tangible. The more we drank, the better the deck looked, and our praise of our work went from the mildly effusive to the frankly ridiculous. I felt that our relationship – which could have gone either way as a result of the exercise – was, like the surface of the deck, significantly strengthened.

"Hum," she said, after a long and enjoyable silence. "I wonder if

we should paint the house?"

I said nothing. I shut my eyes and enjoyed the warmth of the evening sun.

LESSON EIGHT: Efficient communication is a key part of a successful relationship (and silence, appropriately used, is an invaluable component of successful communication). •

Part 3 - Just life

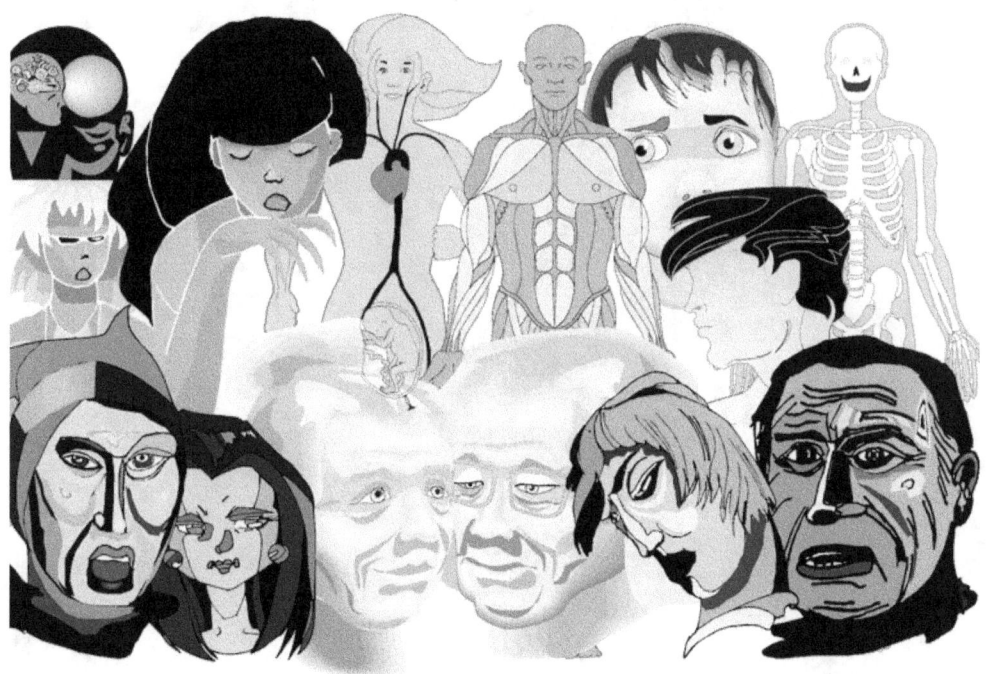

On being an alien

Have you called anyone ugly lately? Or crippled? Or old? Or stupid? Probably not, at least not to their face. We don't do things like that any more, it's victimization. It's accusing somebody of being something that they can't help being. Strange then, that a large proportion of the people who live in the good old U.S.A. are regularly referred to by a term that makes it sound as if they're distinctly unwelcome, as if they're remarkably different, as if they're, well, weird. We call them "aliens."

Like an alcoholic summoning up the courage to admit his addiction, I now stand to say, "Hello, my name is Brian, and I am an alien."

Aliens. What more effective term is there to say "we think you're a bit strange, not one of us, somewhat suspicious"? And yet it's a Government sanctioned term. There are big signs up at airports throughout the land that tell aliens that they have to go somewhere else to be processed, places with longer lines and meaner-faced agents; that they can't use the channels available to other people, people who are non-alien. In fact, you never hear reference to "non-aliens," because non-alien is normal, therefore aliens are abnormal, and because normality is the norm, it doesn't need signs.

In fact, I'm worse than an alien, I have a Green Card, so I'm what the government refers to as a "Resident Alien" which, rather than making me feel like a valuable member of the workforce, makes me feel more like an in-growing toenail. I'm part of the body, but there's something wrong with me. I've erred somehow, deviated, and I've become maliciously embedded in the organism that hosts me, like a toxic parasite. I'm tolerated, but not enjoyed, something about me needs to be fixed, and it's not something that I'm in control of fixing. The only people who can make me whole, make me welcome, make me non-alien, are that most alienating of government departments, the feared INS.

Incidentally, the INS has been renamed the USCIS, or United States Citizenship and Immigration Service. Why the renaming? Who knows? But I bet it cost a lot of tax dollars, some of it alien tax dollars. And why do they refer to themselves as a "Service" when "served" is the last word that I would think of using in relation to my treatment at the hands of the frosty USCIS ?

And have you ever wondered why they call the document issued by the USCIS a "Green Card" when it's actually quite a nice shade of pink? Well, what color was E.T.? It's a wonder that on my driving license, alongside the terse descriptions of "Sex, Hair, Height, Eyes," there isn't a place to record how many brains I have or where my antennae are located.

Part of the process of graduating from being a mere Visa holder to a Resident Alien (and no, it doesn't sound like much of a promotion, does it?), can involve something referred to as "parole." Yes, really, parole! You've committed a crime (being born outside the U.S.A., I presume). What are you supposed to do whilst on parole? Practice being American, I guess, to see if you can make a good enough job of it. At the end of the parole period I dare say the "parolee" will be hauled back in by the USCIS to see if they've suppressed deviant alien tendencies (which would be "Britishness" in my case); to ensure that they've mastered the art of pronouncing tomato as "tomayto" and not "tomahto"; to check that they've seen enough John Wayne movies; that they're convinced that the U.S.A. won the Second World War single handed; that Elvis is better than John Lennon; that the macho Bruce Springstein would make a much better son-in-law than Elton John; and that dental hygiene is a subject of equivalent importance to nuclear proliferation.

Some people don't care about me being an alien – mainly people who take my money, like the IRS. Ever seen a sign at a supermarket that says, "Non-aliens enter here, all others go and stand at the back of the store amongst the trash bins and wait for ever"? I don't think so.

But how do I stop being an alien? I have to force any subversive nation, such as Great Britain, that might lay claim to my alien body to give up such claims. I must promise not to engage any longer in the disgusting practice of "being British." I will write, one hundred times, in my best handwriting: "I promise not to be British ever again." I will remove any traces of Britishness from my home, from my life, and from my mind – be it conscious, subconscious or unconscious. I will take some classes, and then I will gather with a bunch of other deviants – diseased people who are recovering from such terrible afflictions as "being French", or "being Russian" – and I will wave a little flag bearing a prescribed number of stars and stripes, and I will swear never to be a naughty foreigner ever again, cross my heart and hope to die.

And then, with my "condition" firmly behind me, I will no longer be an alien, and I will be able to vote and actually influence how my taxes are spent (yes, aliens pay taxes without being able to vote, which is a bit like wrongly convicted prisoners paying for room-and-board and for the salaries of the guards that shackle them). Best of all, I'll be able to join the National Rifle Association and buy a gun, just in case any of those damned "aliens" start getting ideas above their station! •

Editor's note: Brian became a US citizen recently, and has erected a 20-foot flag pole in his yard to display the stars and stripes and to denounce his alien-ness.

Word play

There are a lot of words in the English language. The Oxford English Dictionary contains about 290,000 separate entries. Some 200,000 are in common use today. But the average person has a vocabulary of only 20,000 of this 200,000. This baffles me because it implies that if your 20,000 are different from my 20,000, we'll both be English speakers but won't be able to understand a single word that the other person says - although being an Englishman living in America, this happens to me almost every day.

Another interesting fact: the average person uses only about 2,000 of their 20,000-word vocabulary in any given week. I suppose they just save the others – words like quidnunc, i.e. "newsmonger", and axolotl (pronounced aks'o-lot-l), i.e. "the larval form of Amblystoma" – for special occasions, or when trying to impress members of the opposite sex or the same sex. Teenagers probably make do with about 200 words a week, complemented by a comprehensive range of grunts, meaningful stares and angry silences.

Twenty thousand words is a lot of words, not as many as 200,000 (I took advanced math at school, so I say this with confidence), but still a hell of a lot. If you don't think it is a lot, try writing down 5,000 different words. Go on.

If you're still reading this piece you've probably taken my word for it, because it takes the average person about 8 hours to write down 5,000 different words. Anyone doing it will, by the time they've finished, either have forgotten why they're doing it, gone mad, or died, and will never come back to read about why they're doing it.

But even given this mountain of words, there are still some surprising gaps in the most obvious of places. For example, when asked whether you like something, have you ever replied by saying "Well, I don't dislike it"? Why isn't there a single, simple word to describe something that we don't actively like, but nor do we actively dislike? Consider this sequence: like a lot, like, like a bit, dislike a bit, dislike, dislike a lot. There's a glaring gap between "like a bit" and "dislike a bit", but that's one hell of a gap, because it describes how most of us feel about all the people in the world that we don't know (assuming we're not a Hare-Krishna "I love everyone" type nor a Charles Manson "I hate everyone" type). Consigning all the people you don't know to an indescribable category on the "like/dislike scale" is akin to trying to pretend that the Inland Revenue Service doesn't exist. (Try it if you like, but I can assure you it doesn't work, and in fact it positively hurts). There are approximately six billion people you don't know, and yet you can't say how you relate to them!

It gets worse. Try telling someone that you like them a bit. You'd wish you hadn't, because telling someone you like them a bit is almost identical to telling them that you dislike them a bit. Sitting on the fence and telling someone that you neither like nor dislike them is just as bad, because it sends the message that you don't think anything about them, and in this world, particularly in the U.S.A., being ignored is the worst possible thing that can happen to you. It's infinitely better to be hated or ridiculed and famous, than to be loved or respected and ignored – if you don't believe me, ask Monica Lewinsky, or Barry Bonds, or Osama Bin Laden, or just about anyone who appears on daytime television.

Shakespeare was a man of many words. He both wrote a lot down and knew a lot. People who studied his texts have concluded that he used between 16,000 and 30,000 different words. I don't know why some of these word counters have come up with 16,000, some with 30,000, and some with various numbers in between. I mean, we know all the books he wrote – it's not as if he also wrote a few books under pen names like Jean-Paul Sartre or Dean Koontz. Perhaps it's because literary people aren't very good at arithmetic, or maybe they get so carried away with the glorious text that they forget where they are and have to go back to the beginning again, something like "11,047, 11,048, 11,049, 'Shall I compare thee to a summer's day' ... Ah, how beautiful ... Damn! Where was I? Oh well. 1, 2, 3 ..."

Anyway, even Shakespeare found it hard to cover the gray areas. Hamlet was forced to consider only two alternatives, to be or not to be, existence or non-existence. What about partial existence? Most of us live the greater part of our lives in a state of partial existence, such as when cleaning the oven, or watching reality television shows, or watching George Bush at a press conference. So why is such a state so badly served by our language? Similarly, can anyone, for example, adequately describe country-and-western music in one word?

Shakespeare encountered language difficulties quite often, or at least his characters did. Macbeth asked, "Is this a dagger that I see before me?" and then went on to think about whether it was or not, but he couldn't allow for the fact that it might be a spoon that looked a bit like a dagger. It was a dagger or nothing. What a great book Macbeth might have been if the dark Thane had been forced to murder King Duncan with a spoon.

Talking about George Bush and press conferences, now there's an example of a man who's not going to let the limitations of language stand between him and his audience. Dubya can take the simplest words and make them completely unintelligible, and the man does it with such grace that he has to be admired. By the way, can someone please solve the mystery that is baffling millions of us? What on earth are the newcooler weapons that the president often refers to? Are they some sort of bomb disguised as a refrigerator? Or are they just cooler than previous weapons, possibly painted in pastel colors or sporting designer brand logos?

It's terribly ironic that such a great enabler as language, a tool that has taken tens of thousands of years to perfect and which has yielded so many literary masterpieces in the process, still has huge gaps in it. And now, before language has had the chance to correct its omissions, the world has moved on to the biggest bastardization of all, text messaging.

In time, young people will probably learn text messaging and only text messaging. Even such a concise but precise and elegant term as Ciao, muttered through full Latin lips, moistened by a foaming cappuccino, has been replaced by a robotic CU hammered out by a sweaty digit on a cell phone.

In the future, whole lives will be conducted in stunted phrases (OMG*), reducing the number of "words" in the vocabulary to about 50 (404*), the Oxford English Dictionary will go out of business (PU*), and Shakespeare's writings will be confined to museums where they're viewed as meaningless hieroglyphics (FUBR*).

How ironic. All one can do is LOL. Oh well, at least I can laugh at it, but does that mean I'm happy? Well, I'm not unhappy.

Notes for the uncool amongst us:

- OMG = Oh my God
- 404 = Clueless
- PU = That stinks
- FUBR = F&*%ed up beyond recognition •

Juliet in Shakespeare's Romeo and Juliet

"A rose by any other name would smell as sweet."

This is a poetic way of saying that what is important is what something is, not what it is called.

"Tis but thy name that is my enemy;
Thou art thyself, though not a Montague. What's Montague?
It is nor hand, nor foot, nor arm, nor face, nor any other part belonging to
a man.
O, be some other name! What's in a name?
That which we call a rose by any other name would smell as sweet; so
Romeo would, were he not Romeo call'd, retain that dear perfection which
he owes without that title.
Romeo, doff thy name, and for that name which is no part of thee take all
myself."

Killing the snake

Although not a particularly religious person, I greatly admire the economy that God exercised when designing the world and the life forms that exist upon it. At every level of existence, there are just enough creatures to engage in healthy competition, without there being so many that they're constantly vying for the same resources (and driving naturalists nuts by making the differentiation between species an impossible task). For example, there is only one animal like an elephant, only one like a great white shark, only one like a giant anteater, and only one like that greatest nuisance of all, homo sapiens.

Going up a level, there is only one Chevy Corvette and there was only one Jimi Hendrix and one John Coltrane. There are only two colors of wine worth talking about, red and white – God dismissed green and turquoise shades from the scene, and only maintains intermediate colors (e.g. blush Zinfandel) for Philistines who are surely headed in the direction of his competitor.

God keeps a pretty good hold on the purse strings when it comes to avoiding redundancy. Of course, there are exceptions, and I can't for the life of me work out why there have to be tailors' dummies AND politicians, but even then I suppose there are only a limited number of jokes you can make about tailors' dummies.

However, I do have a piece of advice that I would like to offer God: Sir, if you knew you were going to invent women, why did you bother to put rattles on the tails of rattlesnakes?

On seeing a snake, the average woman issues a scream that can be heard five miles away, and on seeing a rattlesnake that radius extends to 15 miles at least. God, you could have saved yourself considerable effort (and snake rattles look like pretty complex things to me) if you'd simply relied on the fact that women are always going to find snakes before men do, and they always do, particularly when the men are sitting in the shade drinking a beer, which is what you designed us (men) to do.

This occurred to me recently when I was confronted with the need to dispatch from our property a rattlesnake, which was sending my girlfriend into a state of complete mental meltdown.

One of my favorite poems is *Snake*, by D.H. Lawrence, in which he recounts seeing a snake in his courtyard whilst living in Sicily, and throwing something at it to frighten it off. The point of the poem is not the snake as much as Lawrence's sense of shame at disturbing the poor creature as it drank from his water trough. He ends the poem by commenting on his panicked reaction (throwing a log at the snake) by writing majestically "I have something to expiate, a pettiness." Ah the wonder of language, but I'm afraid that in my case instinct overcame philosophy, bowels overcame vowels.

Oh, by the way, if there are any Wildlife Protection officials reading this, when I say, "killing a snake", what I really mean is "ushering it gracefully from my property". It's a bit like when you're trying to get rid of boring dinner guests after a long meal. The sort of guests who, whilst they're absorbing your hard earned wine and Cuban cigars at a prodigious rate, regale you with tedious and endless anecdotes that would render a single cell organism comatose. In such circumstances you might feel inclined to whack them with a shovel to get rid of them. Thus did I persuade said reptile to go and seek nourishment elsewhere.

I hated doing it. To begin with I wasn't sure it was a rattlesnake, but with a woman screaming in your ear that it is, and that it's going to kill our cat even if it fails to kill us, and that she can't live in the house, or the neighborhood, or the town, or even the state, or the country if this poor creature isn't sent back to its maker (who made a BIG mistake in creating the damn thing in the first place), then the hapless wielder of the shovel is pretty much out of options, and all that's left to do is deliver the whacks that will make his life relatively peaceful once more.

I had been told by the local "snake disposal experts" (i.e. every-one in the area) that you just chop its head off with a shovel. Then (I was told by one particularly enthusiastic expert) you needed to put the head in a coffee tin and throw it in the garbage because the head is capable of biting and delivering venom even after the demise of the villain when its body is being attended to by the local community of turkey vultures. I didn't believe this, but as so many dinner parties round here end up with snake stories, it's good to have a few anecdotes to tell about dead snakes and live ones, just to keep the conversation going. In my estimation, a good dead-snake story is worth at least an extra glass of wine, possibly two.

However, it soon became obvious to me in respect of this par-ticular encounter, that whoever invented the rubber toy snake had based the design on the individual now confronting me. I won't go into gory detail, but the next few minutes reminded me of that old sketch in a Monty Python film where one of the characters is being chopped to pieces but is still yelling provocatively at his attacker, "Is that the best you can do?" as he loses an arm. "Come on, fight like a man!" as he loses a leg, etc. So it was with my adversary. I put my full might into every blow, but the critter seemed to be as affected as if a gentle breeze was ruffling his brow, causing nothing more than minor annoyance.

This nonchalance on the part of the victim (the victim being the snake, that is, although the mantle of victimization was fast trans-ferring to me) was, needless to say, provoking my girlfriend to heightened levels of hysteria. The snake was fast gaining promo-tion from the merely reptilian to being some sort of devil incarnate, so adept were his measures to completely ignore my attempts to separate his constituent parts. But I experienced some relief when he began writhing (and at between three and four feet long there was a lot of him to writhe), simply because my girlfriend then turned her attention and her commentary to the fact that she was likely to throw up at any moment, leaving me to concentrate on the job at hand and ignore her imitation of the soundtrack of The Exorcist playing in the background.

Eventually it was done, and it was then that the D.H. Lawrence effect started to work on me, except it wasn't a mere pettiness I had to expiate, it was a full-blown, high-energy, shovel-wielding assassination. If through some temporary suspension of sanity I'd just bludgeoned our neighbor's cuddly little dog to death, I would have felt suicidal. But the members of the poor old snake kingdom lack the fluffy, playful, wide-eyed appeal of other beasts – if only they could learn to sway their tails, for example, and not simply writhe or thrash them – and as such, instead of evoking warm, cooing emotions, they evoke heavy objects with sharp edges.

My girlfriend and I went out for the ride on our bikes that the snake discovery had interrupted before it had even started. Later, over a cool beer, we managed to convince ourselves that a severe wound that some animal had inflicted on our cat the previous week was probably down to the deceased snake, and my act was one of both retribution and protection against further injury to the lovable cat. Possible, but far from proven. A bit like executing the first man who fits a killer's description without looking for further evidence.

Killing things, big things, like long snakes, takes one back a few thousand years. I reverted, for a minute or two, to being a primitive savage, reacting brutally to something he didn't understand and that was upsetting his woman.

I'm not happy about what I did, and I doubt if the snake is either, and if there's a God up there, I don't think he will have been too impressed by seeing how quickly I sloughed off civilization and chopped up one of his frightening, but magnificent, inventions. ●

Snake by D.H. Lawrence - an extract

A snake came to my water-trough on a hot, hot day, and I in pyjamas for the heat, to drink there. ...

... The voice of my education said to me he must be killed, ...

... And voices in me said, if you were a man you would take a stick and break him now, and finish him off. ...

... Was it cowardice, that I dared not kill him? Was it perversity, that I longed to talk to him? Was it humility, to feel so honoured? I felt so honoured. ...

... And as he put his head into that dreadful hole, ...

... a sort of horror, a sort of protest against his withdrawing into that horrid black hole, ...

... , overcame me now his back was turned. ...

... I picked up a clumsy log and threw it at the water-trough with a clatter.

I think it did not hit him, but suddenly that part of him that was left behind convulsed in undignified haste. ...

... And immediately I regretted it.

I thought how paltry, how vulgar, what a mean act!

I despised myself and the voices of my accursed human education. ...

... I wished he would come back, my snake.

For he seemed to me again like a king, ...

... And so, I missed my chance with one of the lords of life. And I have something to expiate: A pettiness.

There and back

Intonation is everything. The phrase, "Right, boys!" could mean anything. Spoken cheerily it could be encouraging, as if preparing a group of young schoolboys for fun and frolics. Spoken darkly it could be worrying, as if preparing them for bad news of the "our country is at war with the rest of the world" variety. Coming from Mr. Darkwell, the phrase intimated an unfathomable pit of darkness and suffering beyond belief.

Mr. Darkwell was announcing the beginning of another episode of cross-country running. He was implying that something was in prospect that some (such as the super-fit athletes in the class) would find transcendentally stimulating, and that others (the rest of us) would find infinitely painful, humiliating and pointless, unless, that is, one was planning to make a career out of torment, such as by joining the army or taking a government job.

To me, cross-country running was literally "cross country" running. The countryside was cross. It was awfully annoyed at having schoolboys running across it and pounding its surface with our primitive, plodding, flat-soled, pre-Nike running shoes, and it would get its own back by subjecting us to excruciating pain. Pain that started in the jarring feet and contorting ankles, progressed rapidly up the legs via cramp in the calves, twinges in the thighs and aches in the pelvis, until it came to the queasy stomach, which it made instantly queasier, and then moved on effortlessly to the heaving, burning lungs, which was where the real pain set in, before moving on to run rings around and poke ridicule at the pathetically objecting brain.

Mr. Darkwell was an Olympic athlete, literally – he had won a silver medal in a relay event – and it was constantly drummed into us that Mr. Darkwell had achieved this heady goal, not by innate athletic brilliance alone, but by suffering. Pure, unadulterated suffering. Every morning before school began, he could be seen circuit-training in the otherwise empty school gym. Mr. Darkwell didn't consider his workout complete until it had caused him to throw up. In his frequent panegyrics to our hero delivered at morning assemblies, our Headmaster often referred to Darkwell's self-inflicted vomiting as something he considered to be proof of the man's mettle, and a mettle to which we should all aspire. Needless to say, few of us did. In fact, most of us found the spectacle of the groaning and heaving Mr. Darkwell deeply troubling and not at all cozy. Being sick in order to become something, painted an ominous picture of the world ahead of us, and one that was best ignored and ascribed to the "teachers talking irrelevant, out-of-date garbage" category, which was a big category, almost immeasurable, in fact.

But even those of us with a pathological aversion to strenuous physical exercise, myself included, couldn't resist making at least one ritual visit to the gym to witness the spectacle of Mr. Darkwell driving himself to and beyond the brink of exhaustion, where stomach evacuation ensued. Boys, who would never turn up at school more than a few seconds before the final deadline, boys for whom the image of the gym was categorized alongside that of a Belsen oven in the recesses of their minds, were to be found with their noses up against the windows of the building a full ten minutes before they needed to be on the campus, waiting for the moment when the pounding, pumping, leaping, lunging form of Mr. Darkwell would suddenly stop, stand momentarily erect, fold neatly at the waist so that his torso was perfectly parallel to the ground, hands on hips, then throw up neatly on the floor at his feet. No running in panic to the lavatory for Mr. Darkwell. He spewed where he damn well pleased, even if it did mean him coming out later and mopping the floor so that the first gym class of the day wouldn't be slithering their way around the floor on a film of Mr. Darkwell's stomach contents.

One of my more precocious colleagues hit on the idea that given Mr. Darkwell's fame (he was also a runner-up in the BBC's Sports Personality of the Year contest in 1960 something), then it had to follow that his vomit was equally famous, and we could extract value from Mr. Darkwell's suffering by collecting his sick, putting it in miniature test tubes (easily appropriated from the chemistry lab), and selling it to those who would consider anything attaching to a celebrity (or, in this case, spontaneously detaching itself from a celebrity) to be of great worth.

"I mean," said Sanders, the entrepreneurial genius behind this idea, "it's not like an autograph or a piece of clothing. It's part of him."

"Was part of him," interjected the ever-punctilious Basset.

"Is, was, what the truck does it matter? It's got to be a bloody sight more valuable than something he only touched."

"Good idea," I said. "Once we've exhausted the market for his vomit, we can start collecting his shit. A good sized turd will be worth more than it's weight in marijuana!" I was joking, but I don't think Sanders realized I was, and I can only imagine what contortions his brain went through as he considered the logistics of capturing, bottling and retailing Mr. Darkwell's excrement. I lost touch with Sanders after we graduated from school, but I recently heard that he's running a fast food company.

The fact that Mr. Darkwell took the cross-country running class was, to me at least, a disincentive, but it was only a further disincentive, because I was already disincentivized about as much as one could be. I was okay with sports. I liked soccer, thought cricket was okay and rugby was tolerable, and I was reasonably well-disposed to sporty types (I assumed Mr. Darkwell was an exception, and that most athletes were jovial, naturally gifted types who didn't need to go to extremes to achieve extremes – I was wrong).

But I just didn't see the need to run across the land, fighting hills, and mud, and rain, and cold, and wind.

To make it worse, our running was done in a park that was the home of a large deer herd. When the rutting (mating) season is in full swing, one member of the deer family (I neither know nor care which) makes a really God awful smell, a smell bad enough to make even a cast iron stomach ask questions of the brain. During the pungent rutting season, a part of our running course bore evidence to the fact that many of us had far from cast iron stomachs, and given that running took place in the afternoon, after a heavy lunch of school refectory slop, there was usually plenty of evidence to be dodged around, skipped over or skidded through.

One advantage of running the route quickly, was that as soon as you'd done it, showered (compulsory, and assiduously monitored – cleanliness was right up there alongside sportiness at my school, perhaps even slightly above godliness), you were free to go for the day. This meant that the athletes could be on their way home by 3 p.m. if they were as adept at lathering their lithe bodies as they were at hurtling them around the miles of countryside, and this was a full hour before the normal close of school. But this simply meant that one had to start on one's homework that much earlier, and at my school – where the headmaster's much-repeated motto was "study and sport" – there was always more homework to be done than there was time to do it, so having less free time was actually a virtue, in a twisted kind of way. But I have to say that plodding around a stinking park was not my ideal substitute for drawing optical ray diagrams or trying to understand what the hell calculus was all about.

The big disadvantage of coming in at the back of the field was that you had to share the changing rooms with the petty rebels, the barrack-room lawyers, the amateur anarchists, the kids who made

a virtue of failing because they saw it as rejection of the "system."
The athletes may have been smug, but the committed non-athletes
(those who chose to fail on religious grounds, the religion being
revolution) were far too supercilious for my liking. I failed at running because I hated it, not because I was trying to prove something, particularly since the people the non-athletes were trying
to prove it to (the school masters) didn't give a shit for their petty
demonstrations of individuality. So one day, on a whim, I decided
to run and run and just keep running, no matter what my legs
and lungs and brain told me; just to see what it was like to figure
amongst the winners rather than the losers. And, lo and behold, it
wasn't that difficult after all. But my experiment was short-lived
because it came right at the end of the cross-country season, and the
next sport that we were directed at was cricket, which was not only
okay, but it seemed to be a sport that glorified indolence.

Strange, therefore, that 20 years later I should find myself a committed runner; doing six miles each weekday in 40 minutes or so,
more at weekends, running in half marathons, and actually completing a marathon in almost exactly three hours. How did it happen? I've no clear idea. I suppose I was caught up in the running
frenzy that took hold of the world in the 1980s, and once you get
started, it's unaccountably difficult to stop. Perhaps at some point
the inner child within me, the one who'd been running the show
for the first 30 years of my life, and who, unthinkingly, rejected
running as painful and pointless, gave way to the inner masochist
within me, the shady guy lurking at the heart of all of us (sybarites
apart). He's a cunning bastard, that masochist.

Running got me. My life revolved around it. On the days when
I didn't run I felt guilty, as if I wasn't up for the challenge. On the
days when I ran slowly I felt lazy, as if I was growing old, was on
a slippery slope and soon I'd be dawdling around like one of those

ancient joggers that you see now and again, the ones who seem to be doing little more than shifting from foot to foot and making no perceptible forward motion. On the days when I ran well I felt tired, which didn't make me feel good, but at least it didn't make me feel guilty or lazy. In fact, despite working myself into a state of extreme fitness, I never felt fit. I was too tired to take advantage of my fitness and the only way I would get to experience feeling fit would be to stop running for a day or two, which would make me feel guilty, forcing me to go running … etc. There's a vicious circle in there somewhere. I guess you could say that my regular running route was just one big vicious circle.

Anyway, run I did, for about five years, maniacally. One week I ran 84 miles. As I was completing the 83rd of these 84 I reckoned that running had consumed about ten hours of my life in the past week, more if you add in preparation and recovery time. Ten hours a week, 500 hours a year, 2,500 hours in five years. That's equivalent to a year or more of a full-time job. Did I think that my pounding of the pavements was worth it? I slowed my pace appreciably in the 84th mile. Within a month I was down to running a couple of times a week. Within three months I was an occasional jogger. Within six months I wasn't even that – I didn't fit anywhere on the spectrum of definitions of runner, any more than someone who scratches their head has a right to call themselves a brain surgeon.

I don't run at all now. I cycle regularly, but that doesn't have the same intensity of suffering. It has the marvelous concept of freewheeling and you can do it all sitting down. My attitude to suffering is the same as it was when I was a schoolboy, simply "Why?" I've been there and back, and I'm as wise now as I was when I was a teenager. Thank goodness. ●

Editor's note: Brian has reverted and is now doing triathlons for fun (?)

Quotation by Dean Ornish

"Eating a vegetarian diet, walking (exercising) every day, and meditating is considered radical. Allowing someone to slice your chest open and graft your leg veins in your heart is considered normal and conservative."

Dean Ornish   Source: Extreme Health: The Nutrition Connection

In sickness and in health

I'm frightened when I see what my body does. I simply can't imagine that it can keep on doing it. Why don't hearts just stop every now and again? Spontaneously? For no reason whatsoever? Not because of blocked arteries or some other disease, but just because they feel like taking a break? Just like your computer does when you least expect it. Why don't lungs have a rest from time to time? Who could blame them for pausing for five minutes or so their extremely repetitive task – inflation/deflation, inflation/deflation? Even though they wouldn't have a live body to blow life back into when they returned from their coffee and cigarette break, you couldn't blame them for taking the time out.

And what about all those other bits and pieces, the ones that I can barely spell, let alone understand, like adrenal glands, hormones, spleen, hippocampus, gall bladder? If my car suffers miscellaneous failures in just one of its thousands of parts every few months, why shouldn't my body do the same? Given that my body has a lot more parts than my car, that it had no quality control during construction, and wasn't made in Japan by minutely controlled robots, then I should excuse it for shutting down fatally every few days, not every seventy years.

But my body just keeps on doing what it should do, more or less. Sure, there are some blemishes and minor malfunctions here and there, and despite being reasonably athletic, I seem to have been constructed in such a way, either mentally or physically or both, that the playing of golf, even at the most rudimentary level, is completely impossible for me. But all in all I'm amazed by how it all seems to work.

You need to be sick now and again, simply as a reminder of how wonderful good health is. Of course, a couple of days after you've recovered from your illness you'll be taking the miracle of wellness completely for granted again, until the next time, but at least you'll have had a short, poignant reminder.

You've heard it before. Life is a miracle, and all forms of life are miracles, perfected by thousands of years of increasing perfection (evolution), or by divine inspiration (God), or, if you've really drunk the Kool-Aid, by societal improvements brought about by the political party of your choice. But with all this perfecting going on in the world of nature, in animals, and in the animal parts of us (our bodies, our natural instincts) why is it that our brains are screwed up, and seemingly getting more and more screwed up all the time?

Okay, too big a question. Let's stick with the marvels of the body and that part of the brain that doesn't involve greed, racism, bigotry, paranoia and all those other nasty emotions and reactions that cause so much trouble. Perhaps in a few hundred years we'll recognize that our worst characteristics are diseases of a sort, and we'll be able to view them dispassionately and even treat them as we can treat morbid infections today. But we're not there yet, so back to the physical domain.

My father was hardly ever ill, and if he did succumb to anything, he got over it so fast that it was hard to believe that he'd really been sick in the first place. His colds lasted a day. Flu always was literally of the 48-hour variety, even when anyone else who caught the same strain was laid out for two weeks, or when it was decimating populations in Asia.

Once, at over 60-years-old, he fell out of a moving truck when the door latch failed ("Seat belts? What are they?") – that kept him off work for half a day.

He had a double hernia operation when he was eighty-two. It was his first visit to hospital as a patient, and goodness knows how long he'd been living with the condition before he was bullied into seeking medical attention – estimates varied from three months to

30 years. It seemed that no sooner had the surgeon tied up the last of the stitches than my father was up and roaming the ward, sneaking puffs from an illicit cigar, and was out of hospital within five days.

My father took no exercise that wasn't vital, he ate what he liked and smoked tobacco in some format or other during most of his life.

But despite hardly ever experiencing it, illness terrified my father. He hated being ill, or being near sick people, or discussing illness. His only visits to friends or family in hospital were made at moral gunpoint (i.e. intimidation by his nearest and dearest).

It wasn't just illness that spooked him, normal bodily functions and processes were also subjects that he had no interest in, at best, or to which he was mortally averse. The day I was born (at home, as second children normally were in those days), he had a row with the midwife who had come to facilitate my delivery. My father had been planning to go out and watch a football match whilst my mother got on with the disgusting business of introducing me to the world. He was actually about to step out the door before the midwife realized that what she'd thought to be a joke when he first mentioned it, was a genuine intention. He didn't give in easily – I suspect he hid in some remote part of the house, probably listening to the football results on the radio, while I struggled out of the womb.

So for someone born into an environment where at least one parent was of the belief that the subject of health, or lack of it, didn't exist, it has come as quite a change to move from the U.K. to a place, California, where health is as big a fixation with most of the population as football and cricket were with my father.

I remember the first time I went to a dentist over here. I had to fill in the form that summarized my complete medical and dental record since birth (I'm sure that medical offices put us through this ordeal simply so we won't change doctor or dentist too readily). I got to the question, "Are you happy with your smile?" Whereas I'd dispatched all the other questions with a cursory tick or an approximate date (oh, sure I can remember the exact day in 1989 when I had a wisdom tooth extracted), this one brought me to a screeching halt. Happy with my smile?

In the 40 previous years I'd probably thought about my smile for a total of five seconds, and that was just a wild guess, because I couldn't really remember thinking about it at all; although an aunt saying in the dim and distant past that I had a "strange" smile had obviously registered somewhere in the depths of my juvenile mind. I looked at the receptionist.

"Are you happy with my smile?" I asked her.

"Excuse me?" she said.

"I think it's more important to know what other people think of my smile, rather than me personally," I explained. "So what do you think of my smile?"

"You're not smiling," she said. I was, which told me all I needed to know.

But then I got to thinking about the presumption of a dentist who thought she could single-handedly improve my smile, and from there I went on to meditate upon the value of a smile that could be improved solely by cosmetic dentistry. Aren't smiles meant to portray something deep within us? Friendship, compassion, warmth, humanity, love? Could anyone really think that anything as superficial as a course of tooth re-alignment and whitening would substitute for something lacking at the heart of my personality? "No," I said to myself, laughing it off. But over the course of the next two years, surrounded by facelifts, nose jobs, breast implants, Porches, Rolexes, two million dollar homes and luxury brands too numerous to mention, I changed my answer to "Yes".

I live in a place where health and its sidekick, youth, and their pitchman, appearance, are everything. Looking good, which generally means being young, and almost certainly healthy, are the *sine qua non* of an enjoyable life (which is defined as one in which all those around you think that you look better than they do).

In California, and maybe in other parts of the nation too, such as Florida, health isn't about good fortune, as it was for my father, or about sensible living (moderation in all things being at the top of the list). No, here it's a moral obligation. I expect that it's written into the Unofficial State Constitution (which is probably housed in a porn star's mansion in Los Angeles) that "thou shalt look as good, young and healthy as is humanly possible," regardless of the incongruity of a 60-year-old woman having the pert breasts, firm backside, and tightly sculpted face of a teenager.

If I'd been born in California it would be different. If I'd migrated to this environment when I was 20 or so, I might have adapted and been able to jump on the bandwagon. But at 40-plus, with a lifestyle of careless diet, sporadic exercise (i.e. "if it ain't fun, don't do it"), and just-in-time dentistry (i.e. "if it don't hurt, don't fix it") I was simply too late.

Now I have to play the role of cynic, it's my only refuge from all those beautiful people that inhabit the same places as me. My only solace is that beauty fades, but cynicism goes on for ever. •

Breakdowns, nervous and mechanical

Ihave two reactions to mechanical things. Just two. I either love them or despise them. There are no shades of grey. When my car, for example, is working as it should, I consider it to be a marvel of engineering, a tremendous convenience, an entity that I simply could not live without. When it or any significant part of it is not working, however, I hate it with a loathing that would intimidate Hannibal Lecter.

Whilst finding it something of a miracle that cars work in the first place, I feel no contradiction in being surprised when they don't, and that state of surprise exists in a pure, unadulterated state for no more than several milliseconds before it spontaneously combusts into blind rage.

I know it's not reasonable behavior, and many times have I tried to counsel myself into a more rational approach.

"It works 99.99% of the time," I calmly tell myself. "Surely it's allowed the occasional failure?"

"No it's bloody well not!" I yell back. "Cars are supposed to work, and when they don't, they've obviously joined the secret conspiracy amongst mechanical things to make my life a complete and helpless misery."

Last weekend my lawnmower broke down, out of the blue, converting itself from a saintly servant to a devilish subversive in the time it took the engine to sputter to a smoky stop.

Computers likewise. One minute I can be amazed at how much they can do, and the speed at which they can do it. Then something goes wrong, and the next minute finds me scouring an old tome on Medieval Torture Techniques, trying to decide which method I would like to apply to Bill Gates so as to impose the greatest degree of pain and humiliation on the poor man.

I think back to embarrassing episodes when I have hurled malfunctioning mechanical devices around rooms, gardens, garages, bathrooms and kitchens, scaring the living daylights out of myself and anyone else who has been there to witness my complete nervous collapse.

I know that the mechanical breakdowns themselves are caused by the cold, unemotional, impersonal laws of physics, but in the first few minutes after they happen, I see myself as being victimized by Ford, Honda, Briggs and Stratton, GE, Home Depot, Fed Ex, or anyone else on the supply chain that has brought the wayward device to my doorstep.

I think I know where it stems from, this bizarre and uncharacteristic trait. I come to rely on mechanical devices very quickly, and having done so, my brain hard-wires itself to record that, "This thing does this. I bought it, I look after it (sort of), and the thing's part of the contract is to do what I bought it for and to continue to do it until I don't need it any more." When it fails to fulfil this unwritten bargain, my neurons short-circuit and send me into "rant and rave" mode, which is immediately followed by "huge embarrassment and I hope to God nobody was watching" mode.

I'm not like this with people. People have let me down consistently throughout my life, and I might get angry now and again, but my more normal reactions vary from minor annoyance, to disappointment, to understanding, to complete acceptance, to sympathy, even to believing that it was my fault that they let me down and I'm even more bloody objectionable than I had previously imagined.

My expectations of myself, however, clearly fit into the mechanical objects category. When I fail to achieve something that I know I can achieve or have achieved consistently in the past, I am unremitting in the venom I turn upon myself. This explains why I can't play golf, a game in which a shot I can perform easily one week is completely impossible the next, sending me immediately into orbit. When I hear of keen golfers who have broken their clubs and thrown them into a lake in a fit of rage over a bad performance, I simply wonder why they stopped there and didn't go on to kill their infant children, poison the town's water supply with anthrax, and then commit suicide in the local shopping mall by detonating a Weapon of Mass Destruction attached to their testicles (or equivalent female body part in the case of lady golfers).

So it is that whenever confronted by a new mechanical device I act like a Sumo wrestler, circling and eyeing my opponent from a distance, trying to work out from telepathy and instinct alone if it's going to work or not. Then I lunge at it (completely eschewing the instruction manual, of course) and tussle with the device until it starts doing what it's supposed to do, and then immediately fall in love with it as it disposes of a task in minutes that had previously taken me hours to perform manually and arduously.

But wait, all is not what it should be. The engine is sputtering, or the electric motor is whining, or it's emitting a strange smell, or a previously unknown light is flashing until, ultimately, it stops doing what it's supposed to do and starts telling me through smoke, sparks, electric shocks and, eventually, complete inaction, that it's flaking on me. At this moment the love affair ends as quickly as it began, quicker in fact, and all the things that usually happen over weeks as a conventional love affair grinds to a halt are contracted into a few explosive seconds.

Anger, regret, recriminations, pettiness, resentment, all the usual stuff. The only problem is that the machine doesn't seem to go through any of this. There is no empathy, no reciprocity. It just sits there. In the case of a car, the radiator grill turns into a supercilious smirk. In the case of a computer, inscrutable yet condescending messages transmit icy aloofness – "You must restart now". Restart a relationship? How the hell do you do that, wiping the slate clean and trying to replicate that first, exciting eye contact you made across a bar, after all that's gone on between you?

I have to admit that (as in relationships), I'm not good at regular maintenance. I forget birthdays in the same way that I forget oil changes. I buy flowers about as often as I backup my hard drive. I clean my electric toothbrush as often as I look up PMS on the web so that I can offer my partner more sympathy and understanding. I drive a car until something goes wrong, then I take it to the garage and ask the mechanic to fix the car and re-attach all the parts that have fallen off since the last visit (I thoughtfully pick them up and store them in the trunk as they detach themselves). I suppose this is analogous to storing up all the grievances one has with a partner and airing them once a year, expecting them to be addressed in bulk and hoping for a quantity discount. Sounds reasonable in theory, but in practice?

However, all this apart, where would we be without the mechanical devices that are, by now, so much of our day-to-day lives?

We'd be relying upon ourselves to perform all the functions that they so magically carry out.

We would be walking, instead of driving cars.

We would be taxing our brains, instead of relying upon computers.

We would be scything grass, instead of whacking it with trimmers or cropping it with mowers.

We would be having to go out and meet people, rather than calling them on our cell phones.

We would be having to find our own amusements, rather than simply playing a computer game.

We would be struggling to create our own music, instead of being able to turn on the CD player or MTV or the iPod. We would be laboring to write letters, in place of sending txt msgs.

We would have to experience things, in place of simply watching them on television.

In other words, we would be fitter, more intelligent, stronger, more sociable, more creative, more artistic, more literate and more sensitive.

Thank God for machines!

Thank God for machines? •

Images by Alison J. Macmillan

If you like the images in *No man is an island*, you can view them all year round in a wall calendar or a desk calendar, available from WordisWorth's catalog:

www.WordisWorth.com/catalog/catalog.html

The ebook version of *No man is an island* is in full color. As a purchaser of this print edition, you can get the ebook for free. Just send an email to alison@WordisWorth.com, with the subject heading "No man is an island free ebook", and include your name.

About WordisWorth

Where would we be without words?

WordisWorth.com is the success-seekers' gateway to a full range of free information for personal growth and business development.

WordisWorth's goal is to give you free education in an entertaining way, i.e. edutainment.

It's all in the words.
Be entertained while you learn.

WordisWorth.com is a potpourri

You can find so much at www.WordisWorth.com: fact, fiction, business advice, personal coaching, fitness tips, news, trivia, writing, design and editing services, and more besides. You can get a lot of information for your education and entertainment in one place. You live a busy life, you want to succeed, but you don't have time to use lots of different sources to get relevant information and knowledge. If you've suffered conventional learning through dusty textbooks, with dry jargon and complex information designed to make the author look smart, then you might have switched right off and switched on the TV instead or turned to a magazine.

WordisWorth is your TV or magazine. It is designed to entertain you while you absorb its content. It will help and inspire you to get the most out of work and life and be the best you can be. Theory has informed its look and its content. But there's nothing theoretical in it. We present a non- academic and jargon-free guide to our knowledge and learning. •

You can provide your comments and views on this book by emailing the author Brian, or the editor Alison.

We can let you know when we publish Brian's novels. Just send an email with the subject "Brian's new book", and include your name.

Email: brian@WordisWorth.com or alison@WordisWorth.com

We look forward to hearing from you.

Brian and Alison

www.ingramcontent.com/pod-product-compliance
Lightning Source LLC
Chambersburg PA
CBHW071944170626
46813CB00005B/1817